Magic in the Alley

Magic
in the Alley

Mary Calhoun

Illustrated by Wendy Watson

Atheneum 1972 *New York*

Copyright © 1970 by Mary Calhoun
All rights reserved
Library of Congress catalog card number 77–98607
Published simultaneously in Canada by
McClelland and Stewart Ltd.
Manufactured in the United States of America by
Halliday Lithograph Corporation,
West Hanover, Massachusetts
First Printing January 1970
Second Printing March 1971
Third Printing September 1972

For Shirley, in memory of alleys

Contents

Magic in the Alley

Alley Magic

CLEERY PUT DOWN her slice of raisin bread and rummaged through the trash barrel behind the medicine factory. Such an interesting jumble of bottles, to be thrown away! Aha, that little green one shining down there— She reached for it, balancing on the barrel rim. Just then a man stepped out the back door of the medicine factory.

"Hey, kid, get out of that barrel! That stuff might poison you."

Cleery tipped the green bottle to her mouth, watching the man.

"Hey!"

Cleery laughed. She tossed the bottle back into the barrel and dropped to the ground. Silly grownup. Didn't he think children had any sense? She was only looking for something pretty, some bit of treasure. To find something in an alley—it was like a gift from the fairies, unexpected, unimagined, undeserved. A bit of magic.

Retrieving her raisin bread, Cleery walked on in the alley. She was on her way downtown to buy a jigsaw puzzle but, more important, she was exploring a new alley. To Cleery, the best part of the old town of Cricklewood was the alleys. And today she'd promised herself a new one. Cleery rationed them out to herself. Otherwise someday she'd run out of unexplored alleys, and that would be the end.

For alleys were the unknown places, the secret places, the treasure places. Take a perfectly ordinary town with ordinary houses showing their faces and smooth lawns to the streets, and where in such a town would there be a secret place? Back in an alley, that's where.

Hidden away in the in-between places, the unexpected could happen, something slightly aslant with the everyday world. Maybe a gypsy would creep through the alley, or—some stranger creature that Cleery's imagination kept deliciously veiled in mystery. Once in an alley she'd seen a lonely face at a high, back window, like a captive princess in a tower. It was in the alleys, too, that tramps made marks on back gates to show where other tramps might find a welcome. Cleery always watched for chalk *X*'s on the gates, but she never saw one. There weren't many tramps anymore. Or gypsies. Sometimes, though, a whole block of alley was lined with high, board fences, and then the alley was a set-apart road that no one walked but Cleery, her own road right in the midst of town.

Cleery. She sometimes thought her name was just right for her. True, she was named Clara after a dead grandmother, but when she was a baby, her mother had called her, "My little Cleery," and the name stuck. Some of the children at school called her, "Eerie Cleery," because of the things she imagined and because of her tilted green eyes. But even so she liked it. It sounded like an elf's name.

She saw a woman in a back yard hanging out the wash, and she ducked down, waddling so that her head was level with the top of the low fence.

"Oho!" she called to make the woman look.

"I'm an elf," she muttered to herself. "No, I'm a troll, a stray troll, looking over a fence."

She waddled alongside the fence, head turned, big eyes staring at the woman. The woman stared back, clothespin in mouth, hand up to the line, until Cleery was past.

"Bet she thought she saw a troll!" Cleery laughed. Then she stood up and sighed as she walked on. The woman probably hadn't thought any such thing. Most people didn't even seem to know about trolls anymore.

Once when she was younger, Cleery had decided to be a troll for a whole day. She'd said, "Now I'll be a troll," and she'd really expected to change into one. By magic. All those tales of magic her mother had read to her had always seemed like a history of the best things that had ever happened to people. Knights adventuring against wicked witches, elves spinning golden thread for a poor woman. But she hadn't turned into a troll. Another time she'd tried to change sticks and leaves into fairy wands and gold pieces. She'd wished and wished and waved her hands, but in the end she'd still had nothing but gray sticks and a heap of dry leaves.

Even so, Cleery had never given up believing in magic. One time in a school playground discussion, a boy had said incredulously, "You mean you really believe in fairies?"; and Cleery, whisking her hair over her eyes, had said, "Of course. Just because I've never seen fairies doesn't mean they aren't there."

It wasn't just fairies, though. It was the whole idea of magic. Magic was an unseen power, shimmering just beyond what she could see and touch. Like a wind that hadn't blown yet. Cleery was ready for magic whenever it was ready for her.

She ate the last bite of her raisin bread and gave a skip as it went down. There was nothing nicer than exploring a new alley, with a piece of buttered raisin bread in hand. Especially in summer, that part of August when summer seemed to go on forever.

Cleery crossed the street and walked into an alley behind Main Street. Ahead of her, sticking out over the alley, was a sign, THE ALLEY JUNK SHOP. Below the sign was a window hung with cobwebs, as if the articles displayed had been there from some ancient time. Looking in made Cleery think of the age-grown brambles around Sleeping Beauty's castle, where the princess slept, waiting. Junk? Yes, there were cracked pots and peeling picture frames. But there was also an iron dragon with an evil red tongue, a slim curved saber, a small box of carved wood—strange things. Cleery's feet took her to the door, into the shop.

She could see no people inside, only things. The place was like a dream shop, crowded with fascinating clutter to explore. This was the best find she'd ever made in an alley. She'd seen an Alley Lunch and an Alley Shoe Repair, but never a shop like this. Every counter and table, every bit of floor was covered with objects. Yet the room seemed full of life. Shadows shifted; a fleck of light glinted; things moved just at the corner of her eye. Though when she whirled, there was only a butter churn, or a bit of sunlight glancing off a mirror. Cleery saw that strings of feathers hung over the back of the display window, letting in drifts of light as the air from the doorway stirred the feathers.

She hardly knew where to begin looking. There was a tiny dollhouse with the front open, a stuffed crow that looked back at her with steady glass eyes, and, beyond, a bowl of old stamps. Cleery put her hands behind her, in case anyone was watching—the shopkeeper must be there somewhere. Moving to the window, she studied the long-tongued dragon until a flicker of light over the wooden box drew her attention to it. The wood was dark with age, and there was a look of importance to the box, carved as it was into a mass of leaves. A box for holding, hiding, something important. Cleery reached through the feathers.

The box made a solid weight in her hand, despite its small size. She shook it and heard a clinking of things inside. Then she discovered that the box wouldn't open. There was no clasp on the front, no keyhole, only the carved twinings of vines and leaves. She ran her finger over them, tracing the pattern. And something moved. That piece wasn't a leaf. It was more like an upside-down—she turned it—a 7. The lid flew up.

Cleery sucked in her breath at the sparkles and colors, at the wealth of objects lying on the black lining. There was a shining green stone, a blue china bottle with shivery silver lines crusted on it, a small golden box jeweled on top. The jewels spelled out the words: "Last Magic." On the green stone, gold letters said: "One Wish." And on a golden egg, diamonds, circling the egg, spelled out: "24-Hour Invisibility Cloak."

She'd found a boxful of magic.

Cleery clapped the lid shut. Quickly she looked over her shoulder. No shopkeeper, no one in sight. Cleery squatted on the floor behind the butter churn and bent over the box. She turned the 7 again, and the lid lifted. Yes, there were all the colors and

gold and jewels. And the words. They were real. But the magic—could it be real? It must be pretend, or a box of tricks. Yet underneath she couldn't bear to think it was. The shop was so strange, if anywhere in the world you'd find magic— It had to be. It had to—

There was one way to find out. Cleery looked over the objects and saw a tag tied to the neck of the blue bottle. It read: "For Changing Things. Sprinkle Thoroughly." The lid had holes, like a salt shaker.

"All right, I'll just change something!" Her voice squeaked with excitement.

She looked around and saw the stuffed crow on the counter. Hurrying, before anyone came, she shook the bottle over the bird, and a glittering powder rained onto the black feathers. The powder smelled bittersweet, like incense. Oh, she'd forgotten to say what the crow should change into—"Be a cookie jar," she said hastily, "full of—uh—gingersnaps."

Nothing happened. The bird stood there with a faint sheen of powder on its feathers.

Disappointment settled heavily. Slowly Cleery put the bottle back into the box. Just another time when she'd hoped for magic and—it was a mean trick!

The crow's yellow eye blinked. The feathers lifted, shook themselves, settled onto the back again. The crow stared at Cleery.

Cleery stood frozen. It had—moved.

Fearfully she reached out a hand, touched the bird's neck. She felt warmth under her hand. He was alive! The stuffed crow had changed, all right— to a live crow! She must have said the part about the cookie jar too late. Or had the crow been alive all the time? She was sure his eye had been glass.

"Yes? May I help you?"

Cleery spun around. It was the shopkeeper back at last, a gray-haired woman coming from the rear of the room.

For a moment, Cleery wanted simply to run away with the box. She *must* have it, yet maybe it was antique, too expensive. She had only enough money for the round jigsaw puzzle that was on sale—two dollars and fifty cents.

"Yes! Please—how much—?" She held up the box.

The woman looked at it. "Rather nice, isn't it? I've never been quite sure where it came from. But it won't open, you know. Oh, I guess—a dollar."

Cleery's eyes flicked. Should she tell how to open the box? Most grownups didn't believe in magic. If there truly was magic in the box, it might be wasted.

Reluctantly she said, "If I could get it open, would you charge more?"

The shopkeeper looked down at Cleery's wide green eyes, and smiled. "Honey, if you can get it open, that's your good fortune. No, the price is only one dollar."

It was all right, then. She wasn't cheating. She was meant to have the box. Cleery reached for the money in her pocket. As she moved, she saw the crow close one yellow eye. The crow. If this was magic, then the crow was part of it. She should buy him, too.

"How much for that stuffed crow?"

The woman said, "That dusty old thing must be forty years old. It's been here since I started business, so—we-ell—one dollar. Just to make a sale."

Then it had been a stuffed crow before. Cleery thrust all her money into the lady's hand. "Here's fifty cents extra, and thank you, thank you!" she cried.

Before the woman might change her mind, before the crow moved and spoiled everything, Cleery swept the bird under her arm and ran out of the shop. Behind her the woman called, "Don't you want me to wrap—", but Cleery didn't stop running.

She was soon panting, and she wanted to sit right down with the box, but she made herself wait. She zigzagged through alleys and streets, until she came to her favorite hiding-and-thinking place. It was in an alley near home, a grassy spot surrounded by lilac bushes, at the back of someone's yard, a hidden place, with violets in the spring.

"Huff!" Cleery panted as she crawled into the coolness under the lilac leaves. She set the crow down. Yes, the bird was still alive. It hopped a little, settling its wings that still showed glints of the powder. She watched to see whether it would try to fly away, but it seemed content to stand there, turning its head to look around.

So! Then! Now! The box! Cleery wiped the sweat from her face and rubbed her hands on her blouse. She took the wooden box into both hands, hands damp again with excitement. Slowly she turned the box, looking at it. Bits of light that sifted through the lilac leaves flickered over the box. Magic. There had been times before when she'd almost felt it, breathing behind her shoulder. Sometimes when she looked through a window screen she saw movement in the air and thought it was raining, but when she ran out only the wind was blowing. Yet it was more than the wind she'd seen. Sometimes when she lay in the grass, she felt quakes in the air and sounds like distant music. She'd listen, alert, and there was nothing making the sound. Yet in another way the sounds were there. At night, before she slept, sometimes faces appeared unbidden on the backs of her eyelids, weird faces that she had never seen before. She had always known that magic existed. Now at last magic had appeared, real, touchable, all held in one small box.

Cleery wiped her sweaty hands on her blouse again. She moved the 7. The lid opened.

First Cleery counted. There were seven objects lying on the black lining. Then she examined each piece of magic.

One: the blue bottle for changing things. Cleery unscrewed the shaker top and looked inside, but all the glittering powder was gone, only the faint odor of incense remained. Still, the bottle was beautiful, with its silver lines on the blue. Cleery put it gently back into the box.

Two: the green stone. It might be an emerald, for it flashed in the light that came through the bushes. She turned the stone, gazed into its brilliance, ran her finger over the tiny gold letters: "One Wish."

Three: the golden egg. Cleery read again the circling of diamonds: "24-Hour Invisibility Cloak." A seam showed around one end of the egg, and she unscrewed it. Inside was a blue-gray material, thin and soft as mist. Cleery touched the softness and laughed suddenly, almost hysterically. She? To be invisible?

Numbers four, five, and six were small instruments—a silver spoon, a silver knife and an iron key. Cleery puzzled over them. Tied to the spoon's handle was a tag that read: "Magic Mixing-Jelling Spoon." But how was she to use it? How was she to use any of these things? The knife was a miniature dagger, with jagged lines etched on the hilt. Cleery studied the design but could find no words in it. The third thing was simply a small, old-fashioned iron key, with a hole in the end to fit into a lock. Yet it and the knife must have something to do with magic, to be there:

Seven: the gold box with the jeweled letters: "Last Magic." It was a round pan the size of a lady's powder compact, but it felt very light. Cleery shook it and heard a rustle inside. She was tempted to open the box. But the words said: "Last Magic." They must mean it was not to be opened until all the other magic had been used.

Solemnly Cleery promised, "All right. I won't."

Seven pieces of magic! Cleery stretched and then realized how tensely she'd been crouching over the box. She stretched again, curving sideways, almost purring. "Seven magics," she murmured, "six to go. Eureka!" She could go around invisible, she could wish for anything she wanted—

Cleery stopped. The wish. She must be careful not to waste it, as foolish people always did in stories. She must watch her words and never say, "I wish that—" until she was ready. The best thing would be to wish right away, before she forgot and made a slip. Cleery crossed her legs and put her chin in her hands. In the next moment she knew what she'd like to wish. But would it be greedy? She had so much magic already, and really she would have been grateful for even one piece of magic. Yet it was such a right, such a fitting wish.

Cleery picked up the green jewel and held it in the palm of her hand, smoothed it between her fingers. It felt warm. Slowly she spoke, picking out the words, "I wish that every time I explore a new alley, for the rest of this summer, I'll find something— enchanted."

She rubbed the wishing stone quickly and let out a long breath. There. "Enchanted," yes, that was the right word. Sometimes she'd wondered what it would be like if something magical appeared in an alley. What would happen if a witch came to her back gate? In a witchy world, things would proceed with proper witchery. You'd expect that. But what would happen if an enchanted creature came into Cleery's own everyday world? Now, maybe, she'd know. She'd willingly put the limit, "for the rest of this summer," for she knew a magic adventure couldn't go on indefinitely, but the summer was long and—

Then the crow spoke.

"Cookie jar, indeed!" said the crow.

Crow
Magic

CLERRY DIDN'T MOVE. She stared at the crow, as if she could hear with her eyes.

"I might have ended up a cookie jar for life!" exclaimed the crow, spreading his wings angrily.

It was true. The crow had talked. His voice was a little gravelly, but it was real conversation, not just parrot-talk. *Magic was happening.* There she was, sitting under somebody's back hedge, and a real magic crow was talking to her.

"Are you—" Cleery said, her voice trembling, "are you the enchanted thing in this alley?"

"What?" The bird turned an eye to look at her. "You mean that wish you made? No. You fixed me back in the shop. I could have spoken then, but I thought we'd better get out of there. —Me, a stupid, fat cookie jar! Just why? That's what I want to know!" he demanded, hopping forward.

"The magic, I didn't know whether it was real—" Cleery was a little frightened. The crow might peck her.

"It must be real. Look at me. I'm alive again. And—caw! I'm talking!" He clacked his mouth shut in surprise.

"I know!" Cleery exclaimed. "The magic, why you're the most wonderful crow I've ever seen!"

"True." The crow made a satisfied smacking sound with his beak.

Remembering her manners, Cleery said, "I'm Cleery. What's your name?"

The bird cocked his head. "Guess I haven't got a name," he admitted. "I was just a crow until some idiot stuffed me. Just a free-flying crow."

Cleery couldn't get done staring at him, a crow changed by magic. The powder still shone faintly on his black feathers.

"Well, you need a name," she said. "How about Blackwing?"

"Tah!" His beak snapped scornfully. "Just call me Crow. That's who I am."

"All right, Crow. And I'm so glad to meet you! Though I suppose now you're alive again, you'll want to fly away," she added, the last rather sadly. A magic crow might be a good thing to have around.

"Oh, I don't know." He lifted his wings. "Maybe a little whirl."

The bird stepped to the opening in the lilac bushes. Beyond the hedge, he ran faster and flapped his wings. But he didn't fly up from the ground. He turned and ran again, black-stick legs racing, wings beating. Still he didn't fly up. Cleery watched, puzzled, yet glad he wasn't gone. The crow strode back to her, and his pink tongue showed in his beak.

"What's the matter?"

The beak darted and snapped. "The matter? I'll tell you. I—am—a—crow. And I can't fly!" Black wings hooded up ominously, fierce yellow eye glared at her.

Cleery shrank back. "Why not?"

The accusing eye sparkled. "My wings don't lift me. What did you do to me?"

"I just sprinkled," Cleery faltered.

"And said 'Cookie jar' !"

"Oh. The cookie jar part. Maybe when I said that, it mixed things up, stopped the magic from changing you just right—or something. Oh dear."

Cleery felt terribly guilty. For a free-flying crow not to be able to fly—how awful. And it was all her fault. Then she felt so bad about feeling guilty that she became a bit angry at the bird glaring at her.

Sturdily she said, "Well, at least you're alive now. Would you rather be stuffed? And dead?"

"No." He ruffled his wing feathers. "But you! As soon as you get a piece of magic, you go and botch it!"

"Do you know so much about magic then?"

Cleery snapped.

"No, but if I—"

Cleery put her hands to her mouth, upset at the way they were quarreling. "Oh, Crow, I'm sorry!" she cried. "I am so sorry you can't fly. Please, let's not quarrel."

Crow considered her with each eye, turning his head. Then he let his feathers settle. "Well, all right. Shouldn't expect humans to have any sense. Guess you couldn't help it."

But maybe she could help, Cleery thought suddenly. She had a whole boxful of magic.

"Look, Crow, maybe there's something in the box to help you!"

They bent over the magic charms, and Crow picked through them with his beak. The key? The knife? The spoon? No help. "Need some flying powder; that's what," Crow muttered, turning over the invisibility egg. The Last Magic couldn't be used yet, but the bird urged Cleery to wish again on the wishing stone; so Cleery did, rubbing the jewel. It didn't work, just as she knew it wouldn't, for when magic says: "One wish", that's what it means.

Crow dropped down on folded legs by the box. A little feather fell off his body. "All that magic, and not one thing to help me," he said miserably.

Cleery couldn't bear to see the crow so crushed, all his cockiness gone. She started to stroke his neck, then realized that a proud crow wouldn't want to be pitied. Instead she patted his head smartly and said, "Hey, Crow, let's try something!"

They would go back to the shop, she told him. Maybe there'd be more magic tucked away in the clutter. Maybe some flying powder.

Crow stood up and shook his feathers. It was worth a try, he agreed. Cleery scrambled out from under the lilac bushes, box in hand, and set the bird on her shoulder. The alley was sunny and quiet, and across the way a mass of asters shone gloriously purple. Crow's feet gripped her shoulder, his feathers brushed her cheek.

"Alleys are secret; alleys are mysteries; alleys are magic!" Cleery sang out.

"Right," said Crow. "Quit skipping. You're bouncing me."

As they went along, Crow cheered up despite his troubles. "Good to be alive!" he said suddenly, and, looking about, "Same old kinds of birds around, I see. World hasn't changed much in the forty years since I was stuffed."

To reach the shop, Cleery had to walk along a street, and presently she passed some people. Crow seemed to think he'd have fun with his new ability to talk, for when a man approached, the bird called out, "You walk funny!" The man looked sharply at Cleery, as if he thought the gravelly voice had come from her, and Crow laughed, "Caw haw haw!"

"Hey, don't do that!" Cleery said.

Then a woman was nearing them. Cleery looked

at Crow beseechingly. The bird only winked at her and opened his mouth.

"Cawwwww!" he said, until the woman was past. "Fooled you that time!" He chuckled at Cleery's face.

At the shop, Cleery left Crow on the window-sill, so the shopkeeper wouldn't see that he was alive. But, although Cleery poked and hunted through all the drawers and jars and clutter, she couldn't find another thing that seemed magical. Still, she wasn't surprised nor really discouraged. She'd known all along on whom she was counting to solve Crow's problem. Knobs.

Outside the shop again she said, "Never mind, Crow. I'll take you to Knobs. He's a boy who's got lots of sense. He'll know what to do."

As soon as she'd seen all the magic in the box, she'd known just whom to share it with. Just wait till Knobs saw what she'd found!

But Crow was hopping on the sill and squawking, "Boy! You're taking me to a boy? Don't be crazy, girl. Boys don't like crows! He'll shoot me!"

"No," Cleery said scornfully. "Knobs doesn't like to shoot things. He likes to explore things, like me."

Knobs was her best friend. He was her age, and he lived at the other end of the block from her house.

"Don't worry, Crow, Knobs won't hurt you," Cleery promised. "He'll start thinking, and before you know it, you'll be flying again."

She set the bird on her shoulder and started toward her home alley. Crow sputtered and muttered.

"Just a decent crow, flying along to the cornfield, when, *bang*, that boy shot me! Just a decent stuffed crow, sitting on a shelf, when *pop*, 'Be a cookie jar,' she says. Magic, tah!"

Cleery kept reaching up to smooth his ruffled feathers, murmuring, "Now, Crow. Hush. It'll be all right."

At last they reached the alley behind Cleery's block. At its entrance was an old brick carriage house that now housed cars. Farther along was a vegetable garden and grapevines on a fence. Across from Cleery's house, a man kept rabbits in hutches, But the end they had entered was Knobs' end of the alley, and as usual Cleery could smell cookies baking. She hoped there wouldn't be a lot of kids hanging around the kitchen door. Knobs' mother was the Cookie-Mother. All the mothers in the neighborhood worked out at jobs, Cleery's mother, too, but Knobs' mother stayed home and made cookies. You could always get homemade cookies at her house—peanut butter cookies, molasses cookies, any kind. Sometimes she said, "All the other mothers earn money. Maybe I should start a bakery." But Knobs and Cleery and the others always said, "No, don't! Don't. Just be the Cookie-Mother."

With a Cookie-Mother, you'd think Knobs would be fat, but he was all poles and knobs, like his name. He had a knobby nose and knobby cheeks, knobby knees and long slender fingers. His hands always surprised Cleery, as if he had a secret when she thought she knew all about him. His ears stuck out, and he could wiggle them, with a sleepy, faraway look on his face. Cleery would giggle at the ears with a life of their own, and then look curiously at Knobs' face. She teased Knobs a lot, just to make sure he wasn't one step ahead of her.

Cleery looked into his back yard. Nobody there except Knobs, who sat on the back steps with his bony knees up under his chin, face sober, as usual. He was snicking chips of wood off a stick with his pocketknife.

Cleery crouched a little and crept toward him, weaving her arms.

"I'm going to put a spell on you," she crooned. "I'm going to turn you into a frog!"

Knobs glanced up. "Hi."

She straightened and waved the box. "Knobs! Guess what I've got!"

"A crow!" Knobs' face brightened, and he unfolded from the steps.

"Not only a crow!" Cleery exclaimed. ("Huh!" Crow said indignantly by her ear) "But witches! Fairies! Magic!" She waved the box again. "I've found a whole boxful of magic!"

Knobs came close to look. "What's in it, magician tricks?"

"No, sir, Knobs. It's real magic. Look."

Cleery showed him the things in the box and told him about finding it. Knobs studied the contents, squinted through the green stone, face intent.

"How do you know it's real?" he asked.

"Because it works. See this bottle? Well, this crow was a stuffed crow in the shop, and I shook some changing powder on him, and he came alive, and what's more, he's magic. Say something, Crow."

Crow had been glowering at Knobs from Cleery's shoulder. Obediently he snapped, "Mind your manners, boy!"

Knobs stared at the crow. "Magic!" he breathed. Then, "Is it a trick?"

Cleery shook her head solemnly. "Promise."

"Was he really stuffed and dead? Is he still stuffed with straw or something?" Knobs poked at the bird's breast with his fingers, and Crow pecked them.

"Get your fingers out of my stuffings!"

Knobs stepped back and looked at them both. At last he nodded once, with decision "Well, if anyone could go out in an alley and find magic, you could, Cleery."

That's what Cleery liked about Knobs. He believed in the magic because it wouldn't make sense not to, with the crow and the box, right there before his eyes.

But as she might have known, Knobs had only begun to explore the idea of a boxful of magic. He took it from her and looked at it again, tested the 7-latch, examined the bottom for marks.

"Look at that carving. Perfect," he muttered. "No telling how old the box is. Could be hundreds of years." He looked at Cleery. "How do you suppose a magic box got into a Cricklewood junk shop?"

She shook her head. Who was she to question such a find?

"Maybe because the magic is so old—like it comes from forever," she ventured. "Wouldn't it be right to find it among antiques, things that have been handed down and handed down?"

"All right." He nodded. "But somebody had to make these things. Maybe there really were great magicians long ago. Maybe even Merlin."

Crow put in, "I'll bet a wicked magician made it. Look what it's done to me. How do you know this is good magic?"

Knobs thought about that. "Magic isn't either good or bad," he decided. "It depends on how you use it."

Cleery said, "Maybe God made it."

Knobs smiled for the first time. "Oh, can't you just see God fixing up this box of magic and putting it in the shop for you to find?"

Cleery could. She liked the picture.

"Anyway, Knobs, we're going to have all kinds of adventures!" she said. "Because I've already wished on the wishing stone!"

She told him of her wish for something enchanted in each new alley. They could explore together. Find—

"What about me?" Crow interrupted. "That's

what we're here for. What about me!"

She hadn't forgotten, Cleery assured him. She told Knobs about Crow's terrible problem. Crow bobbed his head and flapped his wings to illustrate.

Cleery concluded, "It's just awful for a free-flying crow. Do you understand that, Knobs?"

He thought awhile. Then he said, "I wonder if *you* understand how awful."

The bird could never be left alone on the ground or in a tree, Knobs said, for a dog or cat might attack him, and he wouldn't be able to fly away. Crow couldn't fly here and there to find his food, so all of his food must be brought to him. As Knobs talked, Crow huddled down.

At last the black bird said very quietly, "The shame of it. Independent crow—helpless. I can't even move off this shoulder without falling, unless someone puts me down."

Cleery looked at the eye next to hers and had to look away. "Knobs! What can we do?"

Politely he asked the crow, "May I examine your wings?" A point of blood still showed on Knobs' finger, where crow had pecked it.

Crow's wings lifted, settled. "All right."

Knobs took the bird and sat on the grass. Gently he felt over the body, moved the wings, squinted at the ends of the feather quills. The wings seemed to be hooked on all right, Knobs said. He'd thought maybe the taxidermist had done something wrong in stuffing Crow, but the wings fitted onto the body

just as any bird's did. They should work.

"If the trouble isn't physical," Knobs reasoned, "then the mix-up in the changing magic is to blame. So it will take magic to get Crow flying again. I wonder—maybe if I wished on the stone—"

He tried, but it was no use.

"Nevertheless," Knobs said, "we still have magic to help Crow."

"But there's nothing else in the box to—" Cleery began.

"Cleery, you wished for enchanted things in the alleys. We've got all kinds of magic coming up. Who knows what we may find. Maybe a fairy godmother or—"

"Of course! Why didn't I think of that! See, Crow, didn't I tell you Knobs had lots of sense?"

Knobs ducked his head and set the bird on the grass.

Crow didn't look impressed with Knobs. He said, "More magic! Next thing they'll be changing me into a buzzard. Or a shoe box." He darted his beak at a seed.

But Cleery cried, "A quest! We'll go on a quest through the alleys of Cricklewood, searching for the right magic to make Crow fly. And like knights on a quest, we'll have adventures along the way. We'll rescue fair princesses, fight dragons—"

"Dragons!" Knobs grinned.

"Yes, dragons! Maybe even a sea monster! And this box of magic will be our sword!" Cleery thrust the box through the air like a saber. "Whenever we have trouble, our sword of magic will help us. And the brave Crow shall fly again!"

Crow stopped pecking to look at her. "Caw! How did I get into this!"

Cleery was suddenly still. She had seen something. She moved into the shadow of the garage, and in the shadow she saw something flicker over the box. She crouched down in the shade and stared at it. A tongue of flame showed in the air just above the carved wood.

Knobs saw it, too. He and Cleery looked at each other. They didn't say anything. Cleery passed her hand through the flame. No warmth, no feeling of anything. Knobs put his hand through the small steady light and shook his head. Cleery held the box out into the sunlight beyond the garage shadow. There, the flame was barely apparent. It reappeared only when she brought it back into the shade.

Cleery remembered how light had flickered over the box in the shop window and under the lilac bush. She had assumed it was only the effect of light and shadow. She looked at her grubby hands holding the box with its companion of flame. It made her think of dirty hands reaching for a rainbow.

"Knobs," she whispered. "What business have we got with magic? It's nice to think of, but to have it!"

There was a silence. Then he said in a low voice, "I know. Just the same, it's here. Shall we throw it away?"

Cleery clutched the box to her chest. "No!"

They didn't discuss the box anymore. Instead, since it was nearly suppertime, they agreed to meet in the morning to start on the quest, to explore the magic. Cleery took the crow and the box, and walked slowly down the alley. She held the box carefully in front of her. There was a difference now, knowing that a tongue of fire was standing over the box, even though the flame didn't show in the late afternoon sunlight. It made what she held in her hands more than a boxful of magical playthings. The magic wishing stone she could hold and use, or the spoon, but the flame was alive. In the shade of a tree she could see it, licking in the air, yet it was completely unexplainable. The flame made real and believable the whole power of magic that lay beyond the box, unknown. Her hands trembled. She stumbled as she walked, watching for the wisp of fire in patches of shade. She forgot the bird on her shoulder.

Crow broke in at last, as she passed the neighbor's vegetable garden. "I'm forty years hungry!" he declared.

Cleery laughed, and it was a relief. "Yes, *sir!*" she said, and pulled off an ear of corn from the end of a row. The neighbor wouldn't mind. She'd have to ask Mother to buy corn tomorrow.

Cleery wasn't worried that her parents would object to a crow in the house. When it came to stray dogs and cats, Mother always said, "Bring home anything you like, but you take care of it!" Mother didn't have time. Dad ran the family shoe store that his grandfather had founded, and Mother worked there, too. She did the bookkeeping and typing and sometimes helped old ladies try on shoes. Saturdays, and in the summer, Knobs' mother was in charge of Cleery, while her mother was at the store. Cleery didn't see much of her parents, but they all appreciated each other when they were together. Sometimes Mother and Dad came home from work tired and cross, but the three of them laughed together often enough.

Cleery was right. At supper, her parents looked at Crow and accepted him without a fuss. Crow didn't say anything, for Cleery had warned him that grown-ups wouldn't understand about magic. She wished she could tell her mother, though, after all the fairy tales Mother had read to her when she was little. But she didn't. However, she did mention that Crow couldn't fly. Dad examined the bird, while Crow silently endured having his wings stretched out. Dad said he couldn't find anything wrong and suggested she take him to a veterinarian the next day. Then her parents went to the living room to read the evening paper. Cleery got the giggles in the kitchen, thinking how Dad would look if he knew he'd been handling a magic bird.

It was Cleery's job to wash the dishes every day, so she put Crow in the back yard cherry tree to peck his dessert. The tree was just outside the window

over the sink, so Cleery could keep an eye on him
without any trouble. Suddenly she heard a squawk,
as something black plummeted past the window.
Cleery ran out, wiping her sudsy hands on her sides.
Crow was lying on the grass, one wing crumpled
beneath him.

"Oh, Crow, are you hurt?" She sprang to him.

Quickly the bird pulled his legs under him and
tried to stand. "Just stay back. I'll take care of my-
self," he said angrily.

Cleery stood where she was. "What happened?"

Crow ducked his head to peck in the grass, turning his back on her. At last he muttered, "Well, if
you must know, I was trying to fly."

"Oh." Oh, poor bird.

"Thought maybe I'd only forgotten how," he said
to the blades of grass. "No use. Clumsy. No lightness."

Watching, caring so much, Cleery realized how
it must feel to be an earth-bound crow, gravity pulling down, weighting. How frustrating to the memory of lightly skimming! And there she'd been standing at the sink, thinking only of the enchanted
creatures they might meet in the alleys.

Gently she lifted the black bird to her shoulder.
"Crow," she said, "the enchantments will be wonderful, but the best part of all will be when you fly."

Back in the kitchen, Cleery finished washing
dishes, while the bird perched in silence on the
back of a chair. Cleery was glad when Crow an-

nounced suddenly, "I must build a nest."

Cleery suggested he build it in her room, thinking he'd be safer there, but carefully saying, "Just until you can fly." And Crow agreed. Under his direction, Cleery gathered nesting materials: twigs, mud, sticks and string. He built the nest on Cleery's closet floor—"Like a little privacy, you know!"— while she lay on her bed in her pajamas, watching him. Crow tucked and twitched the twigs and mud with his beak, poking with his toes to get just the right effect, and a bulky framework began to take shape from the mess on the floor.

"How's that for a nest!" Crow clacked his beak. "Pretty good for a bird who hasn't built a nest in forty years, eh?"

Cleery eyed the clutter in her closet. "It's perfectly wonderful, Crow."

Crow went on poking and plastering. "You're not a bad girl," he said briskly.

Clerry smiled. It was the first nice thing Crow had said to her.

"But you don't know how it is with a crow. Building a nest in a house—that's no way to do." *Peck,* he thrust a twig into the framework. "And being carried around all the time. And being hand-fed! And no swooping and soaring!" Crow hopped in agitation. "And being magic! And talking! That's no way for a crow to do, girl!"

Slyly Cleery said, "That's right. No other crow can talk as you can."

Crow stopped hopping and cocked his head. "I do talk rather well, don't I? Took to it right away, really. Must have learned lots of talk, those forty years sitting around on people's shelves. You like my talk?" he chattered.

"Yes!" Cleery laughed. Dear, funny crow. She jumped off the bed and hugged him. "I like *you*, Crow."

"Caw, get away! Stop that!" He slid through her arms and went back to his building project.

But, when Cleery was asleep and dreaming of castles in the alleys, Crow quietly stepped out of the closet. He made a mighty jump onto the bed and walked to her head. Laying a cool beak on Cleery's cheek, he whispered, "May she enjoy the magic."

Sea
Magic

CLEERY WOKE EARLY and wondered why. Why had she been in a hurry to get this day started? Then she heard a voice in her closet, grumbling, "—to wait and wait!"—mutter—"Cornfields—should have been out at dawn—", and she remembered. This was the day of The First Enchantment. She jumped out of bed, caught a toe in the sheets, hopped to keep from falling, and ran to her window.

She knelt there, looking out, past the tree branches, to the houses and streets of Cricklewood. All looked and felt the same as it had each summer morning, dew shining on the grass, an early-day sweetness to the air, a little dog trotting across a lawn, a car passing on the street. Yet somewhere out there, in one of the alleys, she'd find something

36

enchanted. "Magic is going to happen today," Cleery whispered. "I'll see it!" Her stomach felt nervous, as if she were about to play a piano solo. How would she handle it? How would she measure up to meeting some magical creature? A quickening tingled through her. "I'm coming!" she whispered.

"Huh!" said the crow, who had hopped out of the closet. "I should hope so! Sun's been up for hours. If you'll get out and tend to business, maybe you'll get me into the air yet today."

"Oh, yes, sir, Crow!" Cleery tried to squeeze him, she was so full of eagerness and love for everything in the world. Crow flapped her off, squawking, "Stop that hugging! Birds aren't supposed to be hugged." He skipped across the floor to stay out of her reach. Cleery laughed at the way his black legs scissored.

Then she hurried to get on with the day. While Cleery ate breakfast, Crow hopped in the cherry tree. At last, breakfast was done, dishes washed, parents were off to the store—Dad had said, "Taking the crow to the vet today?", and she'd said ambiguously, "I'll find somebody to help him"—and she could go.

Cleery went to her bottom dresser drawer, where she'd placed the magic box. When she opened the drawer, she saw the single flame in it. She squatted on her heels and looked into the shadows. There were her winter socks, some muddy mittens, a wool scarf with burrs in it. And there was the perfectly carved box with its tongue of fire, a flicker of beautiful mystery. Cleery stared into the light, and for a moment she felt older than herself, as she wondered what the flame could mean. What business did she have, carrying around the fire of magic?

"But it was given to me," she said aloud.

The flame moved with the box as she took it from the drawer, and although its light didn't show when she moved into the sunshine, she knew the tongue of fire was there. She held the box and puzzled over how to carry it through the adventure that lay ahead. Her wrap-around skirt had a pocket big enough to hold the box, but it seemed careless just to shove the flame into her pocket.

Besides, the heatless fire would touch her.

Cleery took a deep breath. "Well—amen!"

Holding out her skirt, she eased the box into the pocket, taking care that the lid and the flame faced inward toward her body. She could feel the carved lid pressing against her. "Ho!" she exclaimed in sudden delight. She ran downstairs to get Crow.

Bird on her shoulder, Cleery raced down the sidewalk to Knobs' house. Knobs was waiting on his front steps with a paper sack.

"Oatmeal cookies," he said, picking up the sack, "in case we get hungry. Have you got it?"

Excitement sparked in Cleery, like the first pop of a kernel of popcorn in a skillet. She widened her eyes at Knobs. "I lost it."

"What!"

"No, silly." Cleery laughed. "See?"

She held open her pocket, and they both looked in at the box. A point of light showed against Cleery's body. Knobs looked from it to her face. She smiled, nodded.

Now the popcorn was dancing all over the skillet. "Come on, let's go!" she cried, and skipped away. "We're off—we're off—we're away!"

"Watch out!" Crow teetered and clung.

"Wait up!" Knobs scrambled after them.

Which alley to explore? Cleery had thought about it, at breakfast. What kind of alley would be a good setting for enchantment, for an enchanted creature, maybe? It didn't matter, she'd decided. Any alley that was new to her would hold something enchanted. The wish promised that. Cleery led the way toward a neighborhood of pleasant homes, some blocks distant.

As they walked, they kept reaching into the sack for cookies. Cleery fed crumbles of cookie to Crow, and Knobs began to question the bird. If Crow was magic, could he work magic? Did he eat corn, or did he eat straw? Was he still stuffed with straw? Could he remember what had happened while he was stuffed? How had it felt to come alive again? Knobs had to explore every aspect of the idea of "magic crow." Just how much like humans was Crow?

"Can you laugh? Would you have to laugh if I tickled you?"

He reached out a finger, and Crow promptly

pecked it.

Cleery laughed instead. "It's tickling you want?"

She attacked Knobs' ribs with ten squirming fingers, and Knobs gyrated around on the sidewalk, laughing.

Crow nodded in approval. "I thought *he* couldn't laugh."

Knobs regained his composure and his solemn face. "That was only a reflex reaction," he said.

But Cleery was looking around, not paying attention to his dignity. "Here's an alley I haven't explored," she said. "Here we are!"

The alley was edged with flower beds and garages, garbage cans and a few low fences, along the back yards. An ordinary alley, Cleery thought, with an enchanted creature in it.

"Hush!" she said.

"Quiet!" said Crow.

"Ssh!" said Knobs.

Slowly, softly, they moved into the alleyway, looking all around. A car in a garage—nothing magical there. A fire burning in an incinerator—no fire-breathing dragon there. A gray cat jumped onto a fence, and Cleery looked at it quickly, but it seemed only an everyday cat.

Cleery stopped and motioned for Knobs to wait while she cocked her head and tried to sense—what was it? She sniffed. The air felt damp against her cheek, and there was a smell, a tang—yes, a saltiness. Now, the looks of things—the edges seemed softened,

as if there were a faint mistiness in the air. She felt
a kind of pulse in her ears, a surge and ebb.

"There's something about," she whispered to
Knobs. "Do you feel it?"

Knobs nodded. He touched his ears and swayed
slightly.

Crow shifted against Cleery's neck.

Cleery began to look closely at things around her.
Magic was there. She had only to find it. Shadows
of leaves made a delicate pattern on a sheet hung on
a line, shifting as the sheet moved in the light
breeze. Cleery watched to see if a figure would take
shape from the shadows. A magical being.

"Look!" Knobs whispered, pointing to the dart
of a red jewel. A ruby-throated hummingbird
skimmed over a petunia bed and hung in the air,
its wings a blur of motion, holding the tiny creature
in place as it dipped into each flower. So fragile and
lovely a thing, it must be enchanted. In a moment
would it become a fairy?

"Flight," Crow murmured. "Strong wings."

At the sound, the jewel darted off to rest on the
clothesline. Wings still, motion ended, it was a plain
little brown bird. Cleery and Knobs let out their
breath in sighs.

They moved on down the alleyway, examining,
ready to whirl at a sound. A woodpile here, a fishpond there, a woman pulling weeds at the side of
her house, a dog asleep under a tree.

And nothing. They reached the end of the alley,

and they'd found nothing enchanted.

"This isn't right!" Cleery cried. Her eyes rested on some sparrows hopping on a garbage can, and an awful thought struck her. "Oh, what if we can't tell! Those little birds might be enchanted, and we wouldn't even know it. Maybe they're really fairies enchanted into birds."

"Or dragons." Knobs grinned.

Cleery would have smacked him, except that she was too caught up in dismay. "But, if that's so, how can we ever know what's true? If anything that looks ordinary might be enchanted—I don't like that! How can we tell what's magic?" She sat down in despair on the alley paving.

Crow started to hop off her shoulder, but Cleery caught him automatically with a hand as she sprang up.

"No, that's wrong," she declared. "I wished I'd *find* something enchanted, so I shall. We'll know the magic when we see it."

Back down the alley they went. It was like being on a treasure hunt, only better, because they knew they'd find the treasure. Knobs shinnied up a drain-pipe to look in a bird's nest in the eaves of a garage, but the nest was empty. Crow hopped and puttered along the alley floor, turning over pebbles in hopes of finding another wishing stone. Cleery prowled the edges of back yards. A row of overturned flower-pots stood on a bench, and she looked under each one.

The air seemed mistier than ever, though the sun shone brightly. She saw things as if through a teardrop. And with the pulse, the beat, there came wisps of music, like the tracings of silvery spiderweb. Cleery felt an aura of Something Else sheening over the alley.

Cleery studied the woman crouching at her weeding. Did she feel it? Might the woman be enchanted into a witch? Or that gray cat she'd seen before, was it a witch cat? Cleery watched the cat as it crept across the grass, sneaking up on something, stalking. Oh, the fishpond. Cleery followed quietly. But the goldfish knew when the cat arrived and poised, trembling, on the rim of the pond. All of the fish slipped down under the lilies to hide. Except one, which pulled itself up and sat on a lily pad. Fish— *sat?* Long golden hair!

It was a mermaid.

At the same instant, the cat flashed out a paw and swiped the creature onto the grass.

"No!" Cleery shrieked.

The cat leaped away, startled.

The tiny thing writhed on the grass, fishtail flopping, and a small wailing voice cried, "Help me!" Cleery knelt by it, lips parted. Yes, truly, it was a mermaid. Pretty face, long hair, arms, rainbow-hued tail—and only five inches long, no bigger than a large goldfish. One of the fish had turned into a mermaid. It was her presence in the alley that was spreading forth a mist of magic, sea magic. Now

Cleery felt in her ears the ebb and surge and spray of waves. Sips of salty air came through her lips.

"How can I help you?" she breathed.

"Ninny! Put me back in the water, of course." The tiny voice tinkled and spattered. "And kill your horrible cat!"

"It isn't my cat." Cleery picked up the mermaid, who felt slippery as a fish in her hand, and hastily set her back on the lily pad.

She stared at the creature. She hadn't thought a mermaid would be so small. Eyes, mouth, tail, everything about the mermaid was exquisitely tiny, yet in perfect proportion.

"What a great funny thing you are," the mermaid said, staring in turn from her own narrow green eyes. Her face became pert with points of dimples as she smiled at Cleery. "Anyway, thank you for saving me. I'm sorry I called you a ninny."

Just then Knobs came running with Crow.

"Another lumbering land-thing!" cried the mermaid. "And a black sea gull to eat me!" She dived into the water.

"What is it?" Knobs called.

"I've found it!" Cleery exclaimed.

Knobs dropped to his knees, and Crow jumped to the edge of the pool to peer into the water where Cleery pointed.

"Down there! See the floating hair? It's a mermaid!"

The mermaid shot to the surface, face indignant.

"You told!" She dived again.

Crow began to hop with excitement. "Mermaids can work magic! Quick! Don't let her get away!"

Knobs sat back on his heels. He whispered, "I can feel the sea."

Crow looked up from peering into the pool and cocked his black head. "So do I."

"It's so strange," Cleery said, her voice soft with wonder.

The three of them looked at each other, as the alley air seemed to surge with the ebb and return, ebb and return of the sea. The misty air tingled with the salt of spray, and Cleery heard trailings of music, like sea gulls' cries, like the song of a mermaid.

Cleery bent to the pool. "Mermaid, come up. No one will hurt you. These are friends."

Goldfish darted at the bottom of the pond, and then the mermaid came slipping up through the water, golden hair drifting like seaweed. She pulled herself onto a lily pad and looked at the boy and the bird. Hesitantly she smiled at them.

"Friends?" She looked beyond them at the yard and the houses, her face bewildered. "What is this place?" she cried. "Where is the sea?" Her tail quivered in the water.

Crow soothed, "Now, little miss, don't be afraid."

The mermaid turned her head at his voice. "Ah, a magic talking bird," she said gratefully. "I feared I'd left my world."

"But you—" Cleery began.

She and Knobs exchanged looks. The mermaid didn't know she'd been a goldfish. She thought she'd always been a mermaid.

Now she was begging, "Please take me back to my sisters. Take me back to the sea." She looked at them with her green eyes. "If you are my friends—" she wheedled.

A child's shout sounded nearby. Knobs said they'd better take the mermaid away before someone scolded them for trespassing at the fishpond. He went to a garbage can in the alley and came back with an empty jar and a crooked nail, which he used to punch holes in the lid. After rinsing the jar in the pool, he scooped some water into it, then took the mermaid in his fingers and popped her in.

She clung to the rim, tail lashing. "What, in the name of Poseidon, are you doing!"

Knobs smiled. "Saving you."

The screen door of the house slammed as someone came out. Knobs screwed the lid on; Cleery snatched up Crow; and they all ran into the alley, ignoring the woman who called out behind them. Down the alley they raced and around the corner, in case anyone followed. When they were far enough away, they stopped and sat down on a street curb. The mermaid, who to Cleery's joy was still there after leaving the alley, was tapping angrily on the glass jar. Knobs unscrewed the lid, and she pulled herself up to the rim.

"How dare you slosh me around like that!"

Cleery leaned close to smile at her. "We're saving you."

The mermaid looked at Cleery. "Well, thank you, Miss Giant," she said wryly.

Then they introduced themselves. The mermaid said her name was Mellaby, and she demanded, no, she begged, her dimples coming out, to be taken back to her sisters in the sea.

Cleery discovered that the taste of sea in the air had come along with the mermaid. The air still tasted of salt and throbbed with waves, and she could almost see the tide scatter and slide away in the street at her feet. She stared at the focus of this magic, this tiny girl-fish, alternately so lovely and so pert. Knobs was intent on her, too, his bony face close to the creature. He started to question her, but Crow hopped to the jar and interrupted.

"Oh, magic mermaid," he said respectfully, "we will help you, if you will help me."

"Oh. Yes!" Cleery had almost forgotten, caught up in the wonder of it all.

Then they all talked, telling about Crow, the bird flapping his wings and squawking about the monstrous thing that had happened to him.

"Hush!" Mellaby cried, hands flung over her ears. She considered Crow with her long eyes. "Enchanted," she murmured knowingly. Her dimples came and went, and at last she said, "Bird, I may be able to help you."

"Caw!" shouted Crow. "I knew you could!"

Cleery, however, wondered how they could help Mellaby. There was no sea near Cricklewood, let alone a magic sea full of mermaids. She laid her hand against the box in her pocket. It was to be their sword of magic for rescuing people on their adventures, yet she could think of nothing in the box that would transport the mermaid to her sea.

But Knobs was reasoning out loud. Cricklewood Creek ran into a river, he said, and the river ran into the ocean. Would that help?

"Of course!" said the mermaid. "Put me in the stream, and I can make a charm that will carry me to the sea."

Once at the stream, she promised, she would reveal Crow's cure. Crow bounded about happily, and the mermaid's tail swished with eagerness.

"But I must have a comb," Mellaby added. "I work my charms as I comb my hair."

Where did one find a comb for a five-inch mermaid? A doll's comb would do. Cleery didn't play with dolls, but Knobs' little sister did. They decided to go to Knobs' house for the comb, then proceed to Cricklewood Creek.

Cleery picked up the jar to carry it carefully, and Crow consented to ride Knobs' shoulder, black wings spread atilt in excitement. Mellaby perched on the jar rim and hummed in such a small voice she could barely be heard. Cleery held the glass to her cheek.

"Could you take us with you to your sea?" she asked softly.

Knobs alerted. "Yes, could you?"

"The sea?" The little mermaid's eyes were points of light, like distant stars. "Listen."

She began to sing, weaving the tracings of music Cleery had sensed into a song without words. Cleery felt water sliding about her body. She was lying on the water, rocking, rocking in the smooth swell of waves. A summer ocean spread all around her to the horizons. Cupped over her was a sky, colored with the pearliness of a shell, deep blue at the edges of the sea, rising to misty pink above, softening into a pale blue in the highest part of the arch. The song spattered with notes, and she seemed to rise and sparkle in a dash of spray. She was flung on a beach, running in the sand, gasping with the exhilaration of salt spray in her nose. Until she realized that the mermaid's song no longer sounded. The sea faded into the misty air of the Cricklewood street.

"I was there," Cleery said. "I was rocking in the waves."

"So was I!" Knobs exclaimed. "Sailing through smacking waves."

"But I was flying!" Crow cried triumphantly. "There was a fresh wind, and I dipped down to skim the water with my wing tips, then up over the sea again. Caw!"

"Take us there again!" Cleery begged.

Mellaby shook her head, hair swirling. "You are land-creatures now."

Cleery watched her feet walk over the cracks of the sidewalk. Yes. But there was a teasing note in the mermaid's voice that roused something in Cleery.

When they reached Knobs' house, Cleery didn't go in to help find the doll's comb. There was something she had to do at home, she said, not looking at Knobs. He should come there when he found the comb.

Taking Crow, she hurried on to her house. There she set Mellaby and the bird on the kitchen counter while she assembled things. From a pantry shelf she got an old goldfish bowl, filled it with water and put it on the kitchen table. From the living-room bookcase, she took a conch shell and a piece of white coral she and her parents had brought home from a holiday at the ocean. She placed these in the gold-fish bowl, then plucked the mermaid from the jar and slipped her into the water of the bowl.

"There now, Mellaby," she said, "isn't that a nice place to stay?"

A mermaid to come home to, to sing to her, to plunge her into the surge and ebb, surge and ebb of the sea.

Knobs came in the back door. He saw the mermaid in the bowl, and looked at Cleery. She raised her chin.

"We could take turns," she said.

"Oh, no!" cried the mermaid. Her voice was shrill and pierced like a needle. She began to sing.

Surf pounded in the kitchen, walls of waves rose and crashed. Cleery felt herself tumbling and choking in water. Yet she could see Knobs swaying dizzily. Then she felt the pressure of the magic box against her thigh. And she was overwhelmed, not by the waves, but by shame.

"Stop," she called to her mermaid. "You don't need to do that."

The crashing died away into a shushing of water. Mellaby sat on the shell, lashing her tail, watching Cleery. Cleery gazed down at the tiny mermaid. To think, this creature no bigger than a mouse could evoke such power. Who would have thought there could be so much magic. Cleery knelt by the bowl, so that her eyes looked level into the green ones.

"I know," she said. "It wouldn't be right. Please —forgive me?"

The mermaid stared back at her, tail still flicking in the water.

Crow broke his silence. "Caw! Girl, what have you done?"

Knobs put a hand on Cleery's shoulder. "Look, mermaid, Cleery isn't really like that."

The specks of dimples appeared in Mellaby's cheeks. "I know it," she said. "Just so she knows it." Her voice still teased slightly, but it was the gentle teasing of a friend.

Cleery held eyes with the mermaid for a moment

more and nodded. Then she jumped up to relieve the tension.

"Well, did you get it?" she asked Knobs.

He gave a quick sigh of relief, too. "Yes. Let's get going."

He pulled the comb from his pants pocket and showed it to Mellaby. It was a plastic thing, set with a few colored beads, very small but still a bit big for the mermaid. Mellaby wrinkled her nose in distaste.

"I am accustomed to gold combs," she said, "but I suppose this will do."

Crow began to flap on the counter. "Ho, for the creek!" he squawked. "Ho, for the sky!"

"Right, you old high-flying bird!" Cleery laughed.

She scooped him onto her shoulder. Knobs put Mellaby back in the jar of water. And they were off for Cricklewood Creek. Once on the way, Cleery wondered what would happen when Crow could fly. Would he go on with them in the adventures in the alleys, exploring the magics in the box? Oh, of course he would. He had to.

Cricklewood Creek ran at the edge of town, some blocks distant. The noonday sun was hot, and it felt good to come under the willows along the water. The little stream flowed quietly there, smooth dark water with mossy rocks along the edge and an occasional bird dipping down to its surface for a fly. It was a shadowed, hidden place of dampness and cool greenery. A fitting place for an enchanted mer-

maid, Cleery thought. Gently she lifted the mermaid
from the bottle and placed her on a cushion of moss
at the water's edge.

Knobs gave Mellaby the comb, and her eyes
sparked like stars again.

"Moving waters," she murmured. "Stillness, a
place for spells."

Crow hopped to her. "Miss, I am ready."

Mellaby regarded him and sighed. She said,
"Black bird, my power is limited. I can only look
into the future and prophesy."

Looking off over the water, humming softly, she
began to comb her hair. "Hmmm," the tune trailed,
and the sound of the sea sighed. Mellaby spoke in
a distant voice.

"Listen well, bird. Seek for your help in your
weather of magic. In it lies the power to make you
as you are meant to be."

Crow looked at her with one yellow eye, turned
his head to stare with the other. "Weather?" He
bent closer to the creature on the moss. "But—can't
you fix my wings?"

Her hair swung as she shook her head. "I don't
know that kind of magic. Only can I prophesy." A
dimple flashed, and she laughed a small ripple. "I
didn't say I could make you fly. I said I'd help you.
And I have. I've foreseen your cure."

Crow lifted his wings, still not able to believe that
he wasn't to fly in a few moments. "But—what is my
kind of weather? How will I recognize it?"

"How should I know? Mermaid weather is soft and gray, but brisk like the sea. Giant weather, now, it goes—" the mermaid puffed her cheeks, "—*boof, bump,* the earth quakes. But crow weather—" She shrugged.

Then, as Crow flapped his wings frantically and his eyes glittered with outrage, Mellaby's face softened. Gently she said, "You will find your own right weather. It exists somewhere. We magic creatures always come to the right end."

She began to run the beaded comb through her hair again. "Now it is time for my own special weather of magic," she said. She combed, long, loving strokes down her hair, and as she combed she began to hum. "Come, weather, come, sea, come, magic, rise to me," she sang. "Come, hummm," the mermaid summoned.

The air grew mistier, and the surf whispered in it. The dark water of the stream stirred, foam feathered the surface. Lifting the willows came a breeze and then a wind, rushing the water into a wave. Mellaby slid from the rock and swam out to meet the wave. Salt tang stung in the air, a sound of roaring, shore-pounding waves filled the dark tunnel under the trees. The mermaid lifted to the crest of the wave and floated there, still chanting. She flung out an arm toward Cleery and called a word, but Cleery couldn't hear it over the rushing of water. Then the mermaid swept away through the tunnel on the white crest. Knobs and Cleery and Crow watched until the wave passed around the bend. The salt smell faded, sound faded, the water stilled in the creek.

"Well—" Cleery breathed.

"Well—" Knobs echoed.

"Well—" said Crow, "I still can't fly."

Weather
Magic

"Just wait till the weather changes. Hmph!"

"Well, it's a clue, a direction, you know. After all we found mermaid weather in one alley. Who's to say what's in another. I'm sure your crow weather is someplace. And Mellaby did foresee that you'd find it. She promised you would."

Cleery smoothed Crow, who was flouncing on her shoulder and digging in his toes rather painfully. They were on their way to Knobs' house, the following Monday morning. Over the weekend parents had kept Cleery and Knobs busy, with chores and outings. Cleery had been impatient at the interruption, yet in a way she'd savored the waiting, knowing that more enchantments lay ahead. At night when she lay in bed, it was a marvel to know that a magic crow was tucked up asleep in her closet, and a magic flame was burning in her dresser drawer. Sometimes she got up and pulled out the drawer to see the blade of fire burning bluish-gold in the dark. Once she passed her hand through it, but only once.

Washing up the picnic dishes the night before, Cleery had asked her mother, "Didn't we read one time about a tongue of flame in magic?" And they'd both wondered whether there'd been a flame involved with some knight's search for the Holy Grail.

Mother had said, "Well—'tongue of flame'—when you say it that way, it reminds me of the tongues of fire that stood over the Apostles' heads when the Holy Ghost entered them—after Christ went to heaven, you know."

"Oh. Unhuh." Cleery remembered hearing about it in Sunday school, one Sunday the winter before. The idea of darting flames over men's heads and a mighty sound of wind around them had lit up a gloomy day for her. Cleery and her parents didn't go to church much in the summer.

"But in magic," she'd persisted.

"Flames, lights," her mother had mused. "Wasn't there something in a Hans Christian Andersen— no, Grimms'—fairy tale about a box with a flame over it and a soldier and a witch? Why?"

"Oh, I just wondered."

In her room, Cleery had found the story in her

old Grimms' book, but it wasn't just what she was looking for. Besides, the blue light didn't stand over a box. And it had nothing to do with seven magic objects. She had opened the box again, and again wondered how the things were to be used. Then she had decided not to worry about them. Magic things seemed to take care of themselves. She had gone to bed, wondering.

Now she had her own box and its flame in her pocket again, her own magic that would lead her into its own special places. She stood on the walk in front of Knobs' house and called him.

"Knobs-sie!"

Presently he ambled out the door, managing to knock both elbows on the frame and thrust a sharp knee through a weak spot in his jeans.

"Don't call me that," he said absently. He called back through the doorway, "Mom, Cleery's here, and we're going for a walk. Cleery, I've been thinking."

She grinned at him. "What's new?"

Knobs wagged his ears at her and went on, addressing himself to the bird. "I've been thinking how to find your weather of magic."

Crow bobbed his head. "Yes, yes?"

The mermaid's alley had a certain atmosphere, Knobs said, damp salt air, the rhythm of the sea, "mermaid weather." So the thing to do was to decide what crow weather might be. Then they'd know it when they'd found it.

Crow pulled back his beak. "Tah! That's silly."

"What is your favorite kind of weather?" Knobs asked patiently.

Crow muttered to himself, but after a bit he got to talking. Cleery and Knobs moved off down the sidewalk, listening to him.

Crow weather? Any weather, he said. Crows live out in the weather all the time. So many kinds of good weather. The old bird spoke more slowly, remembering. Cool dawns, when crows spring flapping off branches, shaking the dew from their wings. Wild, windy mornings for soaring and swooping, gusts riffling through wing tips. Hot summer afternoons in cornfields, black backs soaking in the warmth of the sun. Gray, drizzly days, sitting on fence posts, washing wings in the wetness. Icy, snow-bright days, skipping on frozen ponds in a spatter of crows. Still winter sunsets, winging in black flocks across pale yellow and red skies, back to the pine trees for the night.

"Flying weather," Crow murmured. "All weather is good, when you can fly."

Cleery was silent; Knobs too. After they'd walked a block, Cleery said finally, "Crow, we'll find your weather of magic. I promise. It's here somewhere. It has to be. And somehow our magic will bring us there."

In one section of Cricklewood, there stood very old homes, a few big enough to be called mansions, some with wrought iron fences or stone walls around the grounds, some with open stretches of lawn. Certain of the houses were shaped with a beautiful simplicity, others were curiously ornamented, turrets and balconies appearing surprisingly. In this part of town, streets came in at angles and twisted about, not laid out foursquare. Cleery had explored an alley there once and had come upon a full-sized tennis court, behind one of the houses. The leaf-strewn court had been guarded by a sleepy Saint Bernard dog. The area was a fit setting for the unusual and the unknown, and Cleery and Knobs decided to go there.

When they came to the mansions, Cleery looked down several alleys, hesitating to choose. Then she discovered the right one. It was simply a between-way, high stone walls on either side, with branches spreading over the tops and casting leafy shadows on the alley paving. But the lovely thing about the alley—ah, the unknownness of it!—was that it curved out of sight. The stone walls went straight along for a bit, then followed a bend. Cleery realized that this was the kind of place she'd always hoped for. Not only an alley, but one in which she couldn't see to the end. What lay around the curve?

"Just a blank alley," Knobs said. "Doesn't look very promising."

"Oh, but you can't see around the turning!" Cleery exclaimed. "Who knows—I think we should explore this alley."

They entered the leaf-shadowed alley, between

the walls, looking, listening. Set into one of the back walls, they saw a large wooden door, iron-strapped and locked. Then there was only the cobblestone paving to see and the walls and the tree branches. They came to the curve, followed around it, and still the curve continued. It went around and around, circling in on itself.

"This isn't possible," Knobs declared.

At last the curving alley stopped. A stone wall stood across the end of it, a dead-end alley.

"Well," said Crow. "So much for going around in circles."

"But look." Cleery pointed.

At the bottom of the wall was a small grating of black iron. Cleery and Knobs dropped to their knees to examine it. They saw that it was a gate set into the wall, a gate just large enough for a child to crawl through. Cleery peered between the iron strips into darkness at first, for the wall seemed strangely thick. But beyond the tunnel she glimpsed a garden, trees, and a gravel path. The path led into the trees at an impossible distance, considering the way the alley had been curling inward on itself. Cleery sat back on her heels and looked at Knobs, her eyes shining.

"You know what I think, Knobs? I think the walls themselves are the enchanted thing in this alley. And the walls have curved around to enclose an enchanted forest. We must go in there!"

Knobs nodded in amazement. He looked through

the grillwork again. "Yes!"

But the gate was locked. Cleery lifted the latch, and Knobs pulled and shook the gate, to no avail. Then Cleery remembered something.

"Do you suppose—?"

She took the box of magic from her pocket. For a moment she paused, caught by the reccuring surprise of the flame. Then she found the wooden 7 in the carvings and turned it. The lid lifted. She took out the small iron key, put it to the lock. And it fitted perfectly, slipped home into the lock with the rightness of "two and two are four." Cleery turned the key, lifted the latch, and the gate creaked on its hinges as she pulled it open. She turned to Crow, who was standing on the ground beside her.

"Come, Crow, into the enchanted garden."

The bird stepped through the opening, and Cleery and Knobs crawled after him. Leaves had blown into the space under the wall, so that their hands and knees crept on damp leaf mold. The darkness and heaviness of stone were over them, then they emerged into light.

Inside were trees almost as thick as a forest, yet there was grass tended lawn smooth and a sculptured flower bed. A graveled path led into the trees, and, in the distance, through the branches they saw a section of slanting lead roof and more gray stone, perhaps a great house or a castle. It was as though they'd come upon someone's country estate by the back way, a hidden, unexpected way, through the small gate in the wall.

Something came scrambling down the side of the wall. It was a brown squirrel that must have been sitting up there, watching them. Crow jutted his beak, vulnerable because he couldn't fly away. However, the squirrel ran off along the path, tail high, hind legs flung out in the fun of running.

The path invited. Cleery set Crow on her shoulder, her hand slipped out to cling to Knobs' hand, and they set off into the trees. The woods were very quiet, with only an occasional bird twitter or drifting leaf to accent the stillness. Feet *sshed* on gravel, and Cleery whispered. "Maybe we'll find an enchanter, a magician to help Crow."

They came around a turn in the path, and then they could see more of the house, though it was still in the distance. Wonderfully, there was a tower, a castle tower of stone. Yet it was a very unusual castle tower. The top was rounded and glassed over like an observatory; a weather vane stuck up from a little side spire; and an airport weather sock billowed from another spire. A perfect weather tower, a perfect place for an ancient enchanter.

"Weather tower and magic! Crow, I think we've come to the right place!" Knobs exclaimed, and the bird began to caw in excitement.

Truly it was a perfect enchanted forest, Cleery thought, dark and deep and green. The trees stood straight and tall, with green shadows under them and lines of sunlight slanting down through the darkness, as if pointing to something. At the next bend of the path, the tower was concealed behind the trees. The squirrel appeared again, jumping down from a branch and skittering along the path.

Presently the summer forest seemed thicker, cooler, less sunlight penetrating between the leaves. Cleery shivered. It was becoming almost cold. At last they came to a small clearing in the trees, and in the clearing was a building. It was a round wooden structure with a raised platform and a peaked roof, like an open-air bandstand big enough for only one musician. It would have been as pleasant as the little summer houses sometimes found in old-fashioned gardens, except that gray winter light fell on the house from the sky above the clearing, clouds covered the sun. Knobs and Cleery walked around the building. Steps led up to the platform, which had waist-high walls around it and a high stool right in the center.

"Say!" Knobs exclaimed. His eyes sparkled above his knobby cheeks. "That's the perfect place to sit and think!"

He ran up the steps and sat on the stool.

"Wait a minute," he told Cleery. "I need to think what we'll do when we get to the castle." He cupped his chin in his slender hand.

Cleery sat down on the bottom step, though she didn't really like such a cold place, and took Crow into her lap to stroke his feathers. She didn't see why Knobs had to plan yet, when they didn't know what problems they'd find at the weather tower. Still, Knobs was good at thinking things through.

After awhile she said, "Come on, Knobs."

"All right."

He shifted his chin to his other hand, propped up on his knee. He didn't look at her. Cleery felt uneasy. Knobs was all turned inward to himself, and she didn't like it.

Awhile later she said, "Knobs, hurry up."

"Thinking," he murmured.

Cleery was very cold, and the place was very silent. She stood up. "I'm going just to the next bend in the path, to see how near we are to the castle," she said. "Coming soon?"

Knobs nodded, not answering. When Cleery looked back from the path, a light snow had begun to fall in the clearing, and when she reached the bend she could barely see Knobs in his little tower house through the curtain of quiet snow. It was very curious and rather dreamlike. She couldn't see the castle at the bend of the path, so she walked to the next turn, and then she began to feel a little warmer. There was sunlight ahead, so she walked farther.

"There it is," said Crow, who was riding her shoulder.

There again through the trees was the stone tower with its glass dome. It didn't seem much closer, the path twisted so.

"It's strange, Crow," Cleery said. "Do you notice how warm it's getting?"

Crow fluttered his wings. "Feels good, after that freak snow back there. Feels like good old August weather again. And say! There's a good old August cornfield."

At an angle from the gravel path, a little dirt track led through the trees to rows of corn standing in full sunlight.

"I'm hungry," said Crow, smacking his beak. "Let's step over there a minute."

Cleery saw the brown squirrel on the gravel path. He ran ahead a few steps, stopped to look back at her, ran again. The squirrel was like a guide. They really ought to follow him, she thought. But Crow was flapping impatiently on her shoulder.

"All right, just for a moment," she said.

As they drew near the cornfield, Crow said, "Ahh, feel that sun. Smell that sweet corn. Yum!"

Cleery put him down between the rows of corn, and he hopped to an ear that had fallen from a stalk. While he was busy pecking, she sat down in the dirt and enjoyed the warmth. The sunlight glistened on the bird's black feathers. Cleery watched drowsily as he hopped deeper into the green stand of corn.

"Don't go far," she murmured.

However, the beating sunlight was growing too hot for sleepiness. Cleery moved into the shade of a tree at the edge of the corn patch. She could see just a speck of black crow between the green stalks.

"We'd better go back, Crow," she said.

"—a minute," his voice came distantly.

Cleery began to walk in the shade of the trees to amuse herself. A gleam farther back in the woods caught her eye, something yellow. When she went to see, she found golden beauty. Gold and orange leaves carpeted a glade under the trees, satiny autumn leaves. Cleery rubbed some of the soft, bright things on her cheeks. All about, the trees glowed in autumn colors, an autumn woods in an enchanted place. Her favorite time of year, the fall, better even than spring with its secret violets, or summer with its hearty greenness. Autumn, golden banners, glory time of the year.

Cleery wandered among the trees, scuffing her feet in the bronze leaves, jumping into rustles in hollows. A great golden leaf came drifting, lifting, down on the air. Cleery followed it, ran under it to let it light on her head, then ran on, floating and drifting through the woods.

I'm a leaf, she thought. I'm satin-bright, flaming high, floating down, sliding, rustling. She moved to the hum of her imagining, an autumn leaf.

From time to time, through the autumn whirling, she caught a dreamlike glimpse of Knobs, or Crow, through the trees, Knobs still following a thought behind his curtain of snow, black speck of crow pecking among the cornstalks. The brown squirrel was leaping in the leaves with her now. Once when she saw Crow, the squirrel chattered at her, ran a few steps toward the summer cornfield, ran back to her, chattered. She knew he was trying to lead her, and she murmured, "Yes, I will." But not yet. She was a leaf, dancing, spinning, rustling, rushing on in the flaming woods, most powerful of all the autumn leaves. She was a leaf-witch in her woods, spinning, whirling up heaps of leaves for great bonfires. Oh, the smell of burning leaves in the autumn-flaming woods! Yes, set the leaves afire with her brightness, her power, spinning from pile to pile, touching alight, spinning, burning, burning!

Cleery spun to a dizzy stop and stared at the leaves. They weren't burning. But she *expected* them to flare. What—?

She dropped down and held her head until the whirling madness cleared away. How could she have believed such a thing? She'd really thought— At last, with steady eyes, she looked up, saw the golden woods still beautiful. She'd actually been trying to burn the leaves, destroy the woods.

The imagining, it had brought her to this. She'd been having such a lovely time at first, wandering and dreaming. Surely that couldn't have been wrong. Surely—but—but there had come a point when she'd forgotten—what was it?

The others! Where were Knobs and Crow? She'd completely forgotten them. And the weather tower! How could they have become so sidetracked from seeking help for Crow?

The woods are enchanted, she thought. Something about the woods led me astray, made me forget. She looked at the trees around her, and there was nothing wicked about the beauty. The next thought came, unwelcome: she'd done it herself. She could have stopped, followed the squirrel, but she'd wanted to go on enjoying the woods in her own way, never mind the others.

And now Cleery had no idea where she was. No paths, no graveled walk.

A rustling sounded in the leaves behind her. She turned, and there was the brown squirrel, sitting up on his hind legs, nose wiggling, sniffing.

"Little squirrel!"

Immediately the squirrel set off at a scamper over the leaves. Cleery ran after him, and the squirrel led a straight path through the forest. The trees where he led weren't as bright with color. She could see through the woods more easily. There was something moving, someone running—it was Knobs. And there, from another direction, Crow came running on his black-stick legs.

"Cleery!"

"Crow!"

"Caw!"

"I thought you were lost!"

"Where have you been!"

In the midst of greeting, they all stopped and looked at one another out of corners of eyes. Cleery had the quickest tongue, so it was she who said it.

"We just went off from each other, as if we didn't care. And—I imagined I could destroy," she whispered.

"I saw another crow in the cornfield. He flew away."

"I was so cold, so alone."

The squirrel had led them when they were lost, both Knobs and Crow said.

"But he led me, too!" Cleery exclaimed. "How could that be?"

And where had the squirrel gone? They hunted all about, but he was nowhere to be seen in the dead woods.

"Why, look!" Cleery said. "It isn't autumn anymore."

The tree branches were bare and gray, the leaves underfoot old and dark. It was a winter woods.

"There are all these kinds of weather, yet we aren't finding Crow's weather of magic," Cleery said desperately. "We've got to find that tower."

There were no paths, no squirrel to follow. Crow on her shoulder, Cleery walked and walked with Knobs, watching for the stone tower, but all they could see were bare branches. They were lost in the winter woods. When at last they saw gray stone ahead, they ran, then stopped. The stone wasn't part of the castle, after all. They'd come to the wall around the enchanted forest. Still, the wall was a landmark.

"If we follow long enough, we'll come to the gate and the path," Knobs said. "We'll get to the tower yet."

Cleery tried to match his cheer, for Crow's sake,

but she was remembering how the walls had curved around. Maybe they'd become more lost.

They walked beside the wall, and it stretched straight, but the trees still were winter bare. They walked until Cleery's legs ached, and still there was no gate, no gravel path, no sight of the stone tower. Cleery and Knobs realized they were hungry, and Crow said he was, too. Somehow the corn he'd eaten hadn't seemed to fill him up.

At last they came to something different in the barren landscape. Stepping stones led away from the wall. Or rather, up to it, for the stones didn't lead off into the woods. They started at the edge of the trees and went in a pattern right to the wall.

"It's as if they lead out, not in," Cleery said.

They gazed through the trees, but there was no tower to be seen. Knobs stuck his fists in his pockets and considered the stepping stones, looking from them to the blank wall.

"I think you're right, Cleery. I think they're a way out. And what's more, I think we should go out."

In the alley, he said, things wouldn't be so confusing. They'd be able to find the gate again, with no trouble, and start over. Once they were on the gravel path, they'd hurry; they'd run right to the weather tower.

Yes, Cleery agreed, cheered at last. And she still had the key to the gate.

"You two are dumb," Crow said in disgust. "Just

because there's a walk, what makes you think you can go through the wall? And it's too high to climb over."

"Because it makes sense," Knobs said. "The walk doesn't go there for no reason. There must be stones to press that will open a door or something."

He pressed stones, searched for the lines of a doorway, but found none.

"Hmph!" said Crow.

Cleery stood back and looked at the stepping stones. "Funny, the way they're laid out in a pattern, not a straight line," she commented. "They look like hopscotch squares. See?"

She hopped on the stones. "Right foot, right foot, two feet, left foot—" She followed the pattern precisely, from long experience at hopscotch, right up to the wall.

And found herself in the alley. She'd passed through the wall, Crow on her shoulder.

"Ha!" Cleery laughed. "Hopscotch magic!"

She waited for Knobs to appear. And waited. Surely he'd know what had happened. At last he hopped through the wall, passing through the stone as if it were painted air.

"What took you so long?"

"I stumbled and missed, had to go back and start over."

He said it so solemnly that Cleery got the giggles. Knobs was so serious, even about hopscotch magic.

Then Cleery looked at the alley, and all laughter

disappeared. The stone walls went straight along. She could see both ends of the alley.

"Knobs, there's no gate!"

They looked, searched up and down the straight alleyway, but nowhere in the walls was there a little gate into an enchanted woods. Only trees and houses showed over the walls.

At last Knobs stood still and said, "It's no use. We won't find it because the alley isn't enchanted anymore."

"Why?" Cleery cried. "When we were here before—" She looked at Knobs in despair. "Of course. We've been here before. Now this isn't an unexplored alley. Oh, Crow—"

The black bird stood on the paving at her feet, beak drooping. "I know," he said. "We aren't going to find the weather tower."

There was a silence.

"I did it." It was Knobs talking, watching his foot as he scuffed it on the cobblestones. "It was such a still place, such a perfect place to sit and think, but I didn't have to stay there so long, going deeper and deeper into thinking out an idea. After awhile, I just forgot about you."

"Don't fret," Crow told him, "I did it, too, busy enjoying the sunshine, busy filling my belly."

Cleery nodded, echoing, "I did it, too." She thought again of the brilliant autumn woods, as she bent to pick up Crow. The forest had been so beautiful, so promising.

"So enchanted," she whispered.

They stood in the quiet alley, remembering.

Ghost
Magic

THINGS KEPT INTERFERING. Cleery had a cross great-aunt who came to spend a few days, and Cleery had to stay home to be nice to her, while the great-aunt made testy remarks about little tomboys, who kept crows for pets. "Don't you know a bird in the house means a death in the house?" scolded the great-aunt.

Cleery replied, "No, I didn't know that. My!" And the aunt looked suspiciously at Cleery's too innocent face. Really, Cleery was thinking, Crow doesn't mean death, he means life. He just came alive again this month.

Roused by the great-aunt, Cleery's mother fussed a little about the bird's continued residence in Cleery's closet. She said the lazy old crow would probably learn to fly again soon enough, if Cleery

would just leave him outdoors in a tree. Mother
was short-tempered. She didn't seem to enjoy her
aunt's visit, either.

Then the day after the great-aunt went home,
Knobs was busy with an important baseball game.
The boys liked to have Knobs on their team because
he was a good hitter; he concentrated so singly on
connecting his bat to the ball. Cleery couldn't
understand how he could stop for baseball, in the
midst of magic. Of course, she knew the enchantments would end sometime, and she'd still like being
Cleery, living her life. But right now she wanted to
live with the magic.

"Doesn't baseball seem awfully common in the
middle of magic?" she asked Knobs. "How can you
mix baseball and magic?"

"I don't. Baseball is baseball, and magic is magic."

"And never the twain shall meet!" Cleery
laughed.

They were sitting on Cleery's front steps after
supper, after Knobs had helped to win the ball
game. Crow was hopping under the hedge, pecking
at the berries of an ornamental blueberry bush, of
which he had become very fond. Dusk was spreading through the long summer evening, blurring out-
lines, gray-shadowing trees and the farther reaches
of the lawn. But the feeling abroad was not one of
dying day. Instead, night was waking after the sleepy
heat of the afternoon. A car honked on the next
street, a bird suddenly fluttered from one tree to

another. A stir of air brought the sweet smell of petunias, warmed all day by the sun, and Cleery moved restlessly.

She was thinking about the weather tower in the enchanted forest. Glimpsed through the trees, it had been right there, solid, a fantastic tower possible to reach and explore. And now gone. Perhaps the cure to set Crow flying lay in the tower. Gone. Cleery sighed.

Still, there were more alleys out there, more enchantments possible. A man passed on the sidewalk, walking a small dog. Cleery realized suddenly that that man didn't know that magic was loose in Cricklewood. None of the grown-ups knew or would believe. She felt as if she were living in more of a world than they. And maybe even this "more", these touches of magic she was having, weren't the whole thing. Underneath maybe there was something that could transform the whole real world, transform it by magic into a more complete self. But what was "complete?" . . . How much more than she already saw and touched? The vision blurred. Anyway, enchantments were waiting right now in the alleys. And here they sat. She lifted her head in a surge of impatience.

Knobs must have felt the same, for he spoke her thought. "Why wait until tomorrow? Let's go now, in the night. A night adventure should be something special."

A single bird twittered suddenly, a vibration of

excitement in the gathering dusk.

"Yes!" Cleery jumped to her feet, and Crow came running over the grass.

"Now?"

Cleery ran upstairs for the box, called through the hallway, "I'm going for a walk with Knobs," and they left before anyone could object. The night waited, the night alleys, the night enchantment.

At the corner, they passed some children under the street light getting ready to play hide-and-seek in the delicious dusk. The children had grown accustomed to seeing a crow on Cleery's shoulder, and only one ran over to chatter at Crow, while he kept his usual disgusted silence at the silly remarks.

When they were away from the hide-and-seekers, Crow warned Cleery, "Next time somebody says, 'What's new, old bird?', I'm going to tell him!"

"Bet you don't." Cleery rubbed her cheek against his wing, smiling.

Knobs had been silent since they'd started. Now he said wistfully, "I wish I'd found some magic. I mean—well, it's your box, your crow."

Cleery glanced at him out of the corners of her eyes. Knobs wasn't one to be jealous, so it wasn't that. She guessed she'd been running the quest, choosing the alleys, using the magic from the box. Knobs must feel as if he were just "along."

She said, "It was your idea to go at night. Why don't you choose the alley this time, and you use the magic. Let it be your adventure." She handed him the box.

Knobs looked at her in the shadows. He smiled. "All right." He didn't have a pocket big enough for the box so he held it a moment, the flame standing over it, blue-gold in the darkness. Knobs studied the flame for a moment, then he slid the box inside his shirt, next to his skin, and tightened his belt. He stood there silently, his breath coming quicker, looking down at the lump in his shirt. Slowly he put his hand up and pressed the box against him, and Cleery wondered what he thought about the flame touching his skin.

Then, through the dark streets, past pools of light from street lamps, Knobs led the way. Several blocks from Knobs' and Cleery's neighborhood, they passed another group of hide-and-seekers, children they knew at school, and then they came to an area of empty lots, where old houses had been torn down. In one block, only two dilapidated houses still stood. Knobs asked Cleery whether she'd been in the alley of that block, and she said she hadn't.

As they went around to the alley, she eyed the forsaken area. It certainly looked eerie enough for a night adventure. Old fir trees stood black and rusty against the purple sky; a dying cottonwood tree spread bare branches over brick rubble of what had once been a house. Showing in a window of one of the two standing houses was a long square of yellow light. The alley was very dark, away from the street lights.

"So dark we can't even see anything enchanted," Cleery whispered as they entered the alley.

She and Knobs tiptoed, looking nervously from side to side.

"See or not, I *feel* something magical," Crow croaked unexpectedly.

A prickle ran over Cleery's arms. There did seem to be a weather of magic in the alley. Strangely, in the summer night, a wisp of mist floated in a cellar hole by the alley, and over in the field another patch of whiteness hung over the bushes. A creaking sounded as two dead branches scraped together, and Cleery clutched Knobs' arm. There was no breeze to make branches move. The alley began to brighten with a silvery light. Cleery looked around fearfully, and then she saw that a full moon was rising, soft white as dandelion fluff, in the hazy sky.

"Good," Knobs said in a good out-loud voice. "We'll be able to see better."

He looked closely at each thing they passed, Cleery and Crow copying him. They gazed into the misty cellar hole, examined a crumbling stone wall beyond, found nothing interesting behind the house with the single lighted window. Berry bushes had grown wild over the deserted lots, and Cleery looked under the vines along the alley edge, perhaps to find a little enchanted rabbit. She noticed that there were no paths through the bushes.

"You'd think kids would play in these empty lots, but I don't think they do," she commented.

They passed the other house and reached the end of the alley. Knobs turned back.

"Mustn't give up," he said. "Remember how we found the mermaid."

The mist in the alley increased, luminous in the moonlight, and even Knobs hushed his voice. When they came to a stand of gloomy fir trees, Cleery hurried by. She'd rather not find something enchanted right there. They passed through a scarf of fog across the alley. Beyond, Knobs looked up into the cottonwood tree, black sculpture of limbs lifting through the whiteness.

"The mist is even up in the branches," he said. "Hey, there's a treehouse."

The cottonwood was a great old hero of a tree, mighty limbs branching from a massive trunk. High, higher the branches rose, one side bushing with leaves, but most of the limbs dead, twisted bare shapes in the fog. In a crotch of limbs was a deserted treehouse. It consisted of a board platform with sides, one of the sides falling away. Laddering up to the treehouse were bits of wood nailed to the trunk. Knobs tried a toehold on the steps and began to climb, grappling the wide trunk with his arms. As he did, it seemed to Cleery that a black shadow moved in the mist that drifted around the treehouse.

"Just want to look," Knobs said. "Come on."

Cleery followed him up the tree, Crow clinging to her shoulder as she climbed.

She must have imagined the black shadow, for there was nothing alive in the treehouse. It was a good-sized structure, well made in its time, but it looked as though no one had played there for years. A rustling thickness of dead leaves covered the floor, with bits of birds' eggshells mixed in. The mist wisped aside as Knobs hunted around the treehouse.

"Nothing enchanted here," he concluded.

Still, he sat down on the leaves, and Cleery did, too, being careful not to lean against the side that was breaking away. Dead branches around her, drifts of fog in the field—Cleery shivered with excitement. It was something special, to be sitting up there in an unknown tree, in the night.

"I want to see just what magic we have left," Knobs was saying, taking the box from inside his shirt. The flame was the brightest spot in the hazy moonlight.

Crow jumped down to the floor to see, too, and they all looked at the things in the box. The blue china jar, the green stone and the key had worked their magic. Still waiting were the golden egg, the silver mixing-jelling spoon, the silver knife with the strange design on the handle, and the golden box of Last Magic. The golds and silvers glimmered in the moonlight.

"Tonight I use the knife," Knobs mused, "or I stir up some magic, or I become invisible. Ssss!" he sucked in his breath.

"You won't do any of them if you don't hurry up

and find something enchanted," the bird scolded. "Come on, let's get busy!"

Something moved. Something moved on a dead branch farther up in the tree. A faint sound scratched. Cleery started to her knees, and Knobs jumped up, thrusting the box of magic inside his shirt. Then they saw golden eyes gleaming above the branch.

"Just a cat," Knobs breathed.

A slim white cat appeared, hard to distinguish from the mist writhing around the limb, except for the yellow eyes. The cat crept along the branch and started down the trunk toward them.

Crow jumped at Cleery, flapping his wings. "Pick me up. Pick me up! Cats don't like crows!"

But Knobs was whispering, "Cleery. Look again."

Cleery looked and saw that her black shadow had joined the white cat. Its eyes glowed greenly. A pair of cats edged down the trunk, slim white cat and long-haired black cat. But that wasn't the amazing thing.

The amazing thing was that she could see through the cats to the tree trunk.

The white cat leaped, landed delicately balancing on the rim of the treehouse. Now Cleery could hear the black cat purring as it came. Knobs put out a hand, steadied its shaking, reached to the white cat. His hand passed through the outline.

It was as if the cats were—

"Ghosts," Cleery whispered. "Ghost cats." She

covered her mouth with her fingers and stared at the
golden eyes. "Then, Knobs, this must be a—a
haunted treehouse!" Her voice sank away.

Knobs didn't speak. His eyes were big. Crow huddled in Cleery's arms and buried his head in his
feathers. The black cat sprang down to the floor of
the treehouse and with loud purrs began to rub her
fluff against Knobs' legs. Cleery could see the shape
of the cat and the green light of its eyes, and she
could see Knobs' jeans through the cat.

Another sound came from above, a voice chanting, "You can't play in my treehouse. You can't play
in my treehouse." Then it changed, cried brokenly,
"Oh please, please do. Please, play in my treehouse."

Out of the mist in the branches above appeared
long legs. A figure came climbing down the tree, a
girl in a print dress with puffed sleeves and a sash.
Cleery had seen a picture of her mother as a child,
wearing such a dress. Nimbly the girl swung down
through the tree.

And the dark branches showed through the figure
of the girl.

Cleery trembled, understanding at last. The loneliness of the alley, the drifts of fog, the creaking of
branches——in this alley there was ghost weather.
Part of her wanted to climb down from the haunted
tree as fast as she could. And yet—to actually meet a
ghost! Let it all happen, whatever comes, Cleery
thought. She knelt on the leaf-strewn floor of the
treehouse, holding Crow in her arms, waiting. Knobs

stood, waiting.

Lightly the figure stepped down into the tree-house; the ghost stood before Cleery and Knobs. It had a broad, smooth forehead, long hair like strands of moonlight, smudges of dark eyes. The boards and branches showed through its shape. The creature seemed to float over the floor, wringing its hands, twisting bony fingers together.

"At last! At last someone has come to play in my treehouse." The voice sighed like the brushing of leaves in the wind. "I'm glad you've come," she said to Knobs, not looking at Cleery. "What is your name?"

Knobs stared at the ghost. "I'm Knobs. What's your name?"

"I am Elaine," said the ghost-girl. She stopped twisting her fingers and smiled at him.

Cleery giggled suddenly. Here they were meeting a ghost, and it started with introductions, just like the first day at school.

No, it wasn't quite the same. The ghost looked at Cleery with her dark blurs of eyes, and Cleery felt a chill.

The creature said, "I don't like people to laugh at me."

Cleery looked back, very still.

Elaine said to Knobs, "That's how the trouble began. The children laughed at me, so when my father built this treehouse for me, I wouldn't let them play in it."

"You mean when you were alive?" Knobs asked.

Her head bowed, silver hair dipped. "When I was a girl. But now I call to children to come play, just certain ones, you understand, just children that look nice. I call down through the night to them, but they—run." The voice sighed away.

"I'm sorry," Knobs said. "You're lonely, aren't you?" He reached out to pat her shoulder, but his hand went through her. Embarrassed, he pulled it back. "Are you dead now?"

The ghost-girl smoothed her forehead, thinking. "I don't remember dying."

"Well, do you live in a spirit world? I mean, do you go around with other spirits like you? What's it like?" Knobs asked eagerly.

Cleery saw that Knobs was hot on the trail of finding out all about a ghost's life, but the girl took his interest as a compliment.

She smiled at him. "How friendly you are! No, I don't remember a spirit world, either. All I remember is that I used to sit up here with my cats, pretending the treehouse was my castle, and I a captive princess. I'd summon the weather to my tree castle."

Crow's head popped from his feathers. The white cat alerted to the bird, but Crow didn't notice, listening to Elaine.

"I'd say, 'Blow, wind,' and the wind would come and rock the tree. My castle would sway in the wind; and I'd call to the children, 'You can't play in my treehouse'." Her voice rose, wailing.

Knobs glanced at Crow. Intently he questioned Elaine, "Did you really summon weather? Like magic? Could you summon a special kind of weather now?"

"Of course." She tossed her head, hair shimmering in the moonlight. The movement took her drifting over the treehouse floor.

Knobs watched, lips parted in a smile. "How beautiful," he breathed.

Cleery's face seared hot. Knobs didn't have to be so admiring of this ghost-girl.

She said in a loud, flat voice, "I don't believe it."

"Here, here," Crow said nervously. "Let's hope she can!"

Elaine turned her smudgy eyes toward Cleery. Picking up the black cat, she floated over to Cleery and placed the cat on her shoulder.

"You should cuddle my cat instead of that bird," she said. "See how she likes you?"

The black cat purred lovingly as she kneaded her paws in Cleery's shoulder and smoothed her long fur against Cleery's cheek. Then she flashed out a paw to Cleery's head and jumped down, still purring.

"Oh, she scratched me!" Cleery cried, nearly dropping Crow.

Or—at least the paw had reached out as if to scratch. Cleery had felt no touch of the cat on her shoulder at all, no touch of fur on her cheek, no scratch of claw. Yet there was a stinging on her forehead. She felt the place and saw a spot of blood on her finger. Higher in the tree a branch creaked. The cat purred, weaving her ghostly body around Elaine's ghost legs.

"Ah, you're bleeding," Elaine said. "Let me bind it up."

She ripped a strip of cloth from her skirt and tied it around Cleery's forehead, though Cleery didn't want any kindness from this too sweet ghost. The transparent creatures, the mist—so confusing. She couldn't feel Elaine's touch or the cloth, yet her head hurt. Something is wrong, she wanted to say. Knobs, what's wrong?

But Knobs was smiling at Elaine and telling her about Crow. "Could you summon magic crow weather?"

She tilted her head. "Crow weather?" She drew Knobs over to a corner of the treehouse away from Cleery and began to whisper to him. Once she glanced at Cleery, then whispered to Knobs some more. Cleery felt like an outsider. Of course, it was Knobs' adventure. And there was something pitiful about the ghost-girl, in her loneliness. But Cleery didn't trust her.

Knobs came back, his bony face alight with excitement. "She thinks she can help Crow. She says lots of crows come to this tree and—well, come on. She'll show you what to do." He smoothed Crow's back. "Limber up those wings, old bird!"

"Caw! About time!" Crow fluffed out his feathers importantly, and the cats tensed, green eyes and yellow eyes on the bird. Crow muttered to Cleery, "When I can fly again, the first thing I'm going to do is give each of those cats a good peck. Smart-aleck slippery ghosts!"

They had to climb farther up in the tree, Elaine said. She led the way, skimming from branch to branch. Knobs scrambled after her, and Cleery was left to climb as best she could with the burden of Crow. Watching the graceful ghost, she felt clumsy as she swung up to the next limb. The dead branches creaked but held firm. Even as high as they were, the tree trunk was massive. Presently Elaine pointed to a large opening in the trunk.

"The weather hole," she said. "Out of that hole I shall summon the magic weather." Her voice rose in a chant. "Hold the bird inside the hollow of the tree, and I will make magic crow weather flow over him. Earthling, obey! I have spoken!"

Cleery glowered at the ghost. Who did she think she was? But Knobs motioned for her to go ahead, so Cleery sat on the limb and held Crow into the hollow.

In a softer voice Elaine said to Knobs, "Now we must climb higher in the tree. I have another treehouse up there, where I work my weather spells. Come, Knobs."

She smiled at him, pulled his hand, and he followed. Eagerly he questioned her about her life in the tree, and she answered in her sighing voice. Their voices went away as they climbed toward a small platform far above where the top limbs would sway on windy days. Though now only mist hung in those upper parts of the tree. Cleery was left behind in the fog-bound tree. Below her, ribbons of whiteness wound like ghostly branches, and she could see the ground no longer. She felt adrift, as if the haunted tree might not be rooted to the earth anymore but was floating away in the mist. The white cat had slipped upward after his mistress, but the long-haired black cat crouched on the bough beside Cleery and purred. Cleery edged away from the cat, still holding Crow inside the hole.

"It's dark in here." His voice echoed in the hollow trunk. "Don't drop me! How long does this take?"

"Just a little bit," she said, not knowing. "I hope."

Her arms began to feel the strain, and she rested her wrists on the bark of the hole. Elaine and Knobs had reached the platform now. She could see their legs hanging over the edge through the mist. Knobs was having his adventure, all right. But she hadn't thought he'd be having it with another girl, a fascinating ghost-girl. Cleery tried to shake the pain from her head. How silly she was, being jealous of a ghost.

"She must be starting the spell now," she told Crow. "Do you feel anything in there?"

"Only scared. If you drop me, you'll never get me out."

Cleery tightened her hands around the bird. He was heavy, and her head was hurting more. The cat purred beside her, watching, watching her with its green eyes. Above, yellow eyes shone by Knobs' knees. A snatch of Elaine's voice floated down, "— play with me. This branch swings on windy days."

Cleery's head throbbed. A strip of pain pressed around it. Elaine must have bound it too tight. No, that wasn't right, for the strip was only ghost cloth. Cleery felt confused with the throbbing. She wished she could reach up to her head to see if something was binding it, but she didn't dare pull Crow out of the hole, perhaps, just when the magic weather was coming. Besides, if she set him down, the black cat might spring onto him.

The fog, her head, the cat, all seemed a throbbing, purring swirl. She looked up and saw the white cat winding itself around Knobs, or was it the mist? Strands of whiteness wreathed him, like a great cobweb. Yellow eyes showed, as the cat leaped from his knee to the branch below, and a new band of mist stretched from Knobs' leg to the branch. The ghost-girl was a blur in the fog, but her voice lilted sweetly, "—and you'll always play with me in my treehouse."

Elaine was so enchanting. Enchanting! Cleery squinted her aching eyes and tried to think. In a story a fairy maiden had enchanted a knight. *Elaine was enchanting Knobs.* The white cat was weaving mist, binding Knobs to the tree. The pain pressed into Cleery's head, binding it. Pain shot down her arms, her grip on Crow weakened. The black cat

purred.

Cleery opened her mouth, screamed as loud as she could. "Knobs! Pull yourself loose!"

She tried to pull Crow from the hole, to jump up, but the pain pressed, held her there. "Knobs!" she cried up into the thickening mist. Knobs' legs hung motionless from the web of fog. "Play with me," Elaine's voice purred.

Then silver flashed. Something silver moved in Knobs' hand, glinting in the moonlight, slashing through the fog.

"Oh no, no-o-o," came a wail.

The silver knife from the box—Knobs had it, cutting, slashing away the misty bonds of magic that held him. The whiteness began to move away from the upper branches. Now the ghost-girl could be seen standing with her hands flung over her face. Knobs swung down through the tree.

"Cleery, are you all right?"

"The cloth. Cut it from my head," she whispered.

Cold silver touched her forehead, a tug, and the pressure fell away. The pain faded.

Cleery pulled Crow out of the hollow. "Oh, poor bird," she cried. "Crow, I'm sorry."

The cats leaped up through the windings of the tree and disappeared, but Elaine came down, shielding her eyes from the flash of the silver knife. She still wouldn't speak to Cleery. Instead she wailed to Knobs.

"Free me! You have more magic power than I.

I—I don't have power to summon weather. I only said that to keep you here. Free me from haunting this tree," she begged.

Crow made a rude sound with his beak. "Why don't you just quit hanging around?" He stamped on the branch, furious with disappointment.

"I can't stop, as long as I feel guilty," she said, still looking at Knobs.

"Then you have to let go of your treehouse," he told her. "Let anybody play here."

The ghostly figure wavered, as the mist seeped away, then stood white against the branches again. "But it's mine."

"No, not anymore. You're only a ghost."

Elaine moaned, and Cleery was surprised at Knobs' cruelty. But he was watching Elaine. Without looking away, he whispered to Cleery to hurry down the tree and bring the nearest group of children she could find. Cleery protested, afraid to leave Knobs alone with the ghost, but he promised he'd be safe.

So Cleery climbed down the tree, leaving behind Crow, who declared he'd stay to protect Knobs. Two blocks away Cleery found the hide-and-seekers still at play. When she urged, "I've found the best place to play, so hurry before your mothers call you," she was able to lead the children to the tree.

When they reached the alley, it was a place of blacks and whites, silver pools of moonlight and black velvet shadows. Remnants of fog still wisped through the cottonwood tree. Cleery, ahead of the children, could barely make out the whiteness of Elaine next to Knobs on a limb. She saw Knobs touch the ghost-girl, and the shining hair swung as she bowed her head.

"Everyone — all welcome — good-bye — " Cleery heard the sigh.

Then the figure drifted up into the last strands of mist in the top of the tree and went out of sight. The fog disappeared. Elaine's spirit no longer brooded over the tree.

"See the wonderful climbing tree?" Cleery said to the children. "It has two treehouses. And a deep hollow. Just wait till you try sitting in a treehouse in the moonlight."

They hesitated. "But it's always been scarey here. Fog at night." Still, there was no mist then. Only moonlight shimmered in the old tree. "Yeah, great! Beat you to the top!" And the children swarmed up into the branches.

Later, on their way home, Cleery, still a little jealous of Elaine, asked Knobs what had happened while she was gone. All Crow would say was "Huh!", and Knobs said only that Elaine was a very lonely ghost.

Then he looked up, and his musing voice quickened. "Cleery, you know how, at the beginning, you said we'd go on a quest through the alleys and have all kinds of magical adventures along the way, and the box would be our sword? Well, in a way, I did rescue a captive princess tonight."

Knobs' face looked so uplifted that Cleery didn't dare say the things she thought about the "princess."

However, Crow gloomed all the way home. "Summon weather! Fake!"

Laughing Magic

"AND I SHALL do magic, tra la!" It was a happy sort of morning.

Bringing the box to her bed, Cleery took out each object of magic. Sparkles of sunlight glanced off them—such a marvelous lot of magic! She smoothed each piece: wishing stone, changing jar, silver knife, key, all fulfilled in their work; mixing spoon, cloak, Last Magic, still promising. It was the cloak she was eager for today. Morning sun warm on her head, Cleery picked up the golden egg.

To do something magical herself, that's what she wanted. She'd seen magic happen, met magical creatures, but it was as if she was still a bit outside the main flow of magic. She wanted to be absorbed into it, to be magical, too. Invisible!

Excitement fizzed up like bubbles of pop and flowed over as she cupped the small egg. She read off the diamonds encircling it: "24-Hour Invisibility Cloak." Should she? Yes! Cleery unscrewed the end. It was still in there, mistiness of blue-gray, twilight caught up in an egg. Cleery plucked at the softness and pulled it out, lighter than tissue, until it pooled on the bed, a mist of twilight material.

She sprang from the bed and held up the cloth. It was a cloak, all right, a transparent cape with a hood. It felt filmy yet strong, as though it could never tear. It felt—not like any material she'd ever touched. Cleery swirled the cape around her, soft as a breath on her shoulders.

There was a mirror over her dresser. Cleery whirled around to it, then hushed with the solemn moment. Slowly she raised her head and looked.

"Oh—my!"

She was invisible, except—Cleery spurted into enormous giggles. There was her head, floating in the air by itself. Below it the mirror showed the wall, a heap of yesterday's clothing, but no body. Cleery laughed at her face in the mirror. "Goodbye!" She pulled up the hood, and her head disappeared.

"Oh, lovely, lovely!" She skipped before the mirror, and she couldn't see herself at all. Ouch—she bumped her hip on the chair. Which only made her giggle more, for it proved that she was solid enough. People could hear her and feel her, but they couldn't see her. Invisible!

Stirrings sounded in the closet. Cleery flung off the cloak and dropped it on the bed. Hurrying the rest of the magic things into the box, she put them back in her dresser drawer.

Then, voice lilting with sweetness, she called, "Crow, dear, come here. I have something to show you."

The bird walked out of the closet, gaping his beak and stretching his wings. He looked at her suspiciously.

"What are you up to now?"

"Why, Crow, I just want to try something." She picked him up and swung the cloak around her. "Now look in the mirror." She held the bird under the cloak.

"Caw! Where am I?"

Cleery began to giggle again. "You're right here in front of the mirror. Can't you see?"

"No!" Crow struggled out of her arms and jumped to the dresser top. "There I am." He pecked the mirror, stared into it, and turned to look for Cleery. "But where—?"

Laughing, Cleery pulled off the cape. "We were invisible! See, it's the cloak of invisibility."

"Huh!" Crow eyed the misty stuff. "That's quite a trick. Let's try that again."

Cleery obliged, draping the material over Crow on the dresser, so that he could watch himself disappear. They experimented further. When Cleery

sat in her chair, Crow reported that he could see
the chair but not the girl. Then she took her hairbrush under the cloak, and it became invisible. But
when she put the hairbrush on the bed and folded
the cloak over it, the brush and the bed sheets could
still be seen. The invisibility worked only when
something alive was inside the cloak. It swirled
about Cleery's feet and hid them, and her hands
were not visible when she held them outside, as
long as the cloak covered her shoulders. But her
head did show, if she didn't keep the hood pulled up
over it. Cleery thought of the tales of disembodied
heads floating in the air. Could the heads have belonged to people wearing invisibility cloaks? She
whirled in the cape, with just her head showing.

"Think of all the fun we'll have today! Wait till
old Knobs tries this!"

But the bird stopped still on the bed and glared
at her. "Just—one—minute. What about me? What
about hunting my weather of magic?"

"Oh, but, Crow!" Cleery bubbled with certainty.
"This is such a happy, good day. Don't you feel it?
I just know we'll find your magic today."

Crow submitted to being carried down to breakfast, muttering that *he* wasn't all that sure; but
Cleery chucked him under his beak and told him to
put on a happy face, to be ready to fly.

Breakfast dishes washed, Cleery gathered up all
of her magic—the box, the cloak and Crow—and ran
down the sidewalk to Knobs' house. She began to

chuckle. Stopping in front of his house, she put on the cloak and covered her head. But she left Crow sitting on her shoulder outside the material.

"Knobs! Come out!"

Knobs reacted satisfactorily. "Wha—" His mouth stayed open at the sight of Crow sitting on nothing in mid-air.

Cleery snaked an arm from under the cape and pulled the bird beneath it.

"Crow!" Knobs shouted. Then he recognized the giggle. "Cleery, what are you doing?"

Letting down the hood of the cape, Cleery danced her head in circles around Knobs, laughing. "It's the twenty-four hour invisibility cloak!"

Then she took it off and showed it to him. Knobs was fascinated, but he had to scold her a little first.

"You shouldn't pull an invisibility cloak off, right out here in the street. You might give somebody a heart attack. This is the way you should do it."

Knobs took the cape, looked all around, then stepped behind a tree. He put his head out to say, "I feel like Superman." Knobs was trying to seem casual, but his face was tense with anticipation.

Then—"Ta daaa!"

Cleery started. She hadn't heard Knobs step from behind the tree. It was a weird feeling, to have someone walk around invisible, not knowing where he was. It had been different, when she'd put the cloak over Crow, because she'd known he was right there. She felt for Knobs, but he was being tricky, not making a sound as he moved. Cleery never did find him, until he stepped around the tree, holding out the cloak in his hand.

"That is very, very nice," Knobs pronounced. And he grinned in a very unKnobslike way.

Then they got down to the business of finding the right alley for Crow's weather of magic. As they walked, Knobs said maybe Cleery shouldn't have taken the cloak out yet, for they might need it some other day. But Cleery refused to worry.

She interrupted him. "Here's a pretty alley. Doesn't it actually look happy? It's just what we need."

The alley was dappled with sun and shade, and along one back yard ran a low stone wall with roses climbing on it. There were thickets of trees on the alley; the backs of the garages were neat; and farther along there was a grape arbor. Cleery could hear birds singing in the trees, a fresh, sweet sound. She smiled at Crow, who had lifted his head to peer, and smoothed the black feathers so near her cheek.

"Crow," she said, "this is a place for happy magic. Be ready. And I'm going to be magical right away!"

Knobs took Crow, and Cleery whisked the cloak around her. She clasped it at the throat, and the last Knobs saw of her was the sparkle of her green eyes. As they advanced into the alley, Crow ran out his tongue, trying to taste any mysterious change in the weather. Cleery skipped ahead of Knobs. It gave her a gay dizziness, not to be able to see herself skipping. How delicious it was to be magical and to know that an adventure would begin any moment, yet not to know what it would be! They might meet a blue fairy in the grape arbor. Or a dragon, slithering its length down the alley. Maybe in that cluster of ceramic lawn figures a duck would become a goose that laid a golden egg.

The weather was so sunny and lifting, Cleery sang out, "Today is the day that Crow will be flying!"

The weather? Yes. Cleery cocked all her perceptions. There was a feeling of gaiety, bounce and swing. But maybe that was in her. No, there was more. In the darting breeze, she sensed a quick rhythm ticking in synocopation—"Tick-itty-tick." She clicked her tongue to it. And then she heard wisps of laughter, teasing, chuckling, not from a certain spot, simply in the air.

Cleery ran back to Knobs and Crow. "There's a weather about! What is it?"

Knobs looked toward her voice and grinned. "I hear something laughing, but it's hard to know whether it's magic or you."

"Caw haw!" Crow hopped on Knobs' shoulder. "I feel like laughing, too. Hey, girl, it's laughing weather!"

If it was happy weather, then it must be a good omen for Crow's cure, they all decided. Every step, they watched for some enchanted creature, some magical thing. Birds chirped, breezes whisked, and the ticking rhythm bounced in the air.

Cleery saw something move in a vegetable garden at the alley's edge. There were rows of green beans climbing poles, and as she stepped between them she saw an older girl gathering beans. Cleery crept closer and tossed a few beans into the girl's bucket. She choked back her giggles as the girl looked at the bucket in surprise. Cleery tiptoed away, feeling like a fairy godmother who'd almost appeared to Cinderella.

Yet, on along the alley, nothing enchanted appeared. Knobs and Cleery retraced their steps, watching. Something teased at Cleery. Something was missing that she'd seen before. From the corner of her eye she saw a movement, like the dart of a mouse. Whisks of teasing laughter sprinkled in the air. It wasn't a mouse she'd seen. It was a tiny man.

Cleery knew then what it was she'd missed: a ceramic dwarf was no longer shooing the flock of ceramic ducks.

The creature had slipped under a bush and was grinning, seeming to think he was unseen. He was a little old man, no more than a foot tall, in a dusty gray jacket and peaked green hood. He had a wrinkled face, but with his bright eyes, upspringing eyebrows and wispy whiskers, he looked like a Scotch terrier ready to romp.

Cleery knelt down by him. "Hello. Are you a dwarf or a troll?"

The little man perked and stared around. "Just

an honest English elf, ma'am. Hodge is the name. Are you a witch?"

"Oh. No. I'm Cleery." She took off the cape and pointed to Knobs, who came running. "And that's Knobs, and that's Crow."

Crow's eyes glittered at the sight of the wrinkled elf. "Hello there! Say, mister, can you—"

The elf nodded to the now visible Cleery. "I see. A sorceress, her magic rook and her lackey. At your service, Ma'am."

"Lackey!" Knobs' eager face became indignant. "Rook?"

"A rook is an old-fashioned sort of English crow," Cleery whispered to the bird. She told the elf, "Knobs is no lackey. He's the brains of the group."

"Right," said Knobs. He waggled first one ear, then the other, at the little man, who watched the performance with interest.

"Very good," said Hodge. "I never could learn that trick." Somehow his small voice was both squeaky and gruff.

Crow jumped down to the grass beside the elf, and the two were nearly the same size.

"Look, Mister Hodge, I need your help. I can't fly."

He told his story, and the elf listened, eyes sharp under the spires of his eyebrows, but twice he whisked around in a circle, as if eager to be away. And when Crow was done, Hodge shook his head.

"*I* can't even fly," he said. "Don't know how I

could teach you."

Crow stalked about on the grass in dismay. He tried to make the little man understand that it wasn't teaching he needed.

"Magic!" he squawked. "Make some kind of a spell for me."

The old elf only grinned. "Can't. Get that sorceress to make a spell. An elf's business is helping good workers and tricking lazy ones, and it's time I hopped to it. Nice to meet you, Ma'am."

Hodge tugged at his green hood and disappeared.

Cleery and Knobs stared at each other in a clap of disappointment. Was that all?

"But I was counting on him," Crow said.

Yet there was still a weather of magic in the alley. The tickety rhythm went on in the air, a chuckle spurted now and then, and drops of rain teased, followed quickly by sunlight. Then a dog began yapping furiously in a nearby house.

"He's still around," Knobs said.

They raced across the grass and looked in a kitchen window. There were no people in the room. A little dog crouched by the stove, barking in a frenzy, hair standing up on his back. At the sink, dishes zipped from dishwater to drainer. Invisible Hodge was at work. Three dishes sailed up and down in the air, juggling, as the silverware flew into the drainer. Cleery and Knobs laughed. "Whoops!" Cleery gasped, as a platter nearly hit the floor.

Next, a tide of soapy water swooped across the

kitchen floor from a bucket. And as quickly mopped itself up. The dog scampered away from the water, tail between its legs. In a moment, the floor was shining clean, and then nothing more happened.

"He's gone somewhere else. Quick, track him!" Cleery exclaimed.

Running in and out of people's yards, Cleery tossed the invisibility cloak to Knobs to cover him and Crow, and they disappeared with a shimmer of grayness. People wouldn't fret about a trespassing girl as much as they would about a boy and a crow. She and Knobs clutched hands to keep together, and holding an invisible hand made Cleery giggle so much, at first, she could hardly run.

It was like a game, chasing Hodge through grassy yards, past flower beds, over stone walls, pouncing on a trace of elf here, a bit of elf there. Sometimes the elf popped into sight, grinning and scampering, then tugged his green hood and disappeared again. One time something invisible was digging weeds, dandelions sailing into a golden heap. Then he was hiding! But there was his face, peeping out of the ivy on an old wall. No, he was over there! Peaches flew out of a tree into a basket.

"Wait, Hodge!" Knobs called out. "We need to talk to you."

"He's got to be magic!" Crow declared.

Hodge appeared suddenly, scrambling down the tree. Basket in one hand, he carried it light as a leaf. "But not crow magic!" he said. He winked, pulled at his hood and disappeared.

Over by a pond, a boy let out a yelp. He'd been lying on his stomach on the grassy bank fishing out frogs, dumping them into a jar, while his lawn mower stood idle. Now the jar of frogs emptied over his head, frogs bouncing and springing, squeaky laugh ringing in the air.

Next door, a little boy ran out and pulled a shirt off a clothesline. It was strung with laundry that was stiff and dry, as if it had been there overnight.

"Lazy housewife!" gruffed a voice, whisking away.

Cleery and Knobs followed, to peek in a window and see a woman lounging in front of a noisy television set.

"Hoho!" shouted Hodge's voice.

The clothes on the line began to fly through the air, up into trees, twisting around bushes.

Cleery tugged at the cloak, "Knobs, please?" She flung on the cloak and joined in the fun. She wasn't as quick as Hodge, but she helped decorate the back yard with neglected laundry. Socks bloomed on rose bushes. Aprons festooned the hedge, and sheets draped over the woodpile. Whisk! A pair of jeans went up a tree and stuffed onto the top branches. The legs flourished in the breeze, as if a man had plunged out of the sky into the tree.

Cleery laughed. "Oh, Hodge, that's wonderful!"

Dashing about with the laundry, the elf had bumped into her leg once, and she'd nearly stepped on him. It amused her to discover that one invisible person couldn't see another invisible person. It wasn't as if they were in another dimension. Hodge's power to become unseen seemed to lie in his hood, which he always touched before he disappeared. Crow must have noticed that, too, for when the elf appeared, hands on hips, laughing as he surveyed his work, the bird jumped down from Knobs' arms.

Crow skipped across the grass, calling, "Mister Hodge! I've got an idea for more mischief. Listen!"

The little old man turned eagerly. "What?"

"This!"

Crow darted out his beak and snatched the green hood. Hopping away, he swung it over his own head, gave it a nip with his beak and disappeared.

"Give that back!"

The elf ran to the place where Crow had been, but the bird's voice taunted from another spot.

"Oh, no, Mister Hodge. Now I've got the magic!" His voice became reverent. "Oh, hood, let me fly."

Cleery flung her hands to her face as she watched the air, but a flying bird didn't appear in it.

"Ohh!" Crow's voice moaned.

"Told you it's not a flying hood," the elf cried furiously. "Wait till I get you!"

He darted about on the grass, hands outstretched to feel the bird. Without his hood his ears showed pointed and his hair even spikier than his eyebrows. Cleery began to giggle at the sight of the scurrying elf, being teased in turn.

Crow appeared at the foot of a tree. The hood

had fallen off. Crow pecked up the hood and skittered away. Hodge scampered after him, but just in time Crow cocked the hood onto his head and was gone.

"Black-hearted thief!" Hodge jumped in rage.

"Caw haw!" The laughter of Crow whisked here and there. "Caw haw haw, you can't catch me!"

And no matter how the elf whirled and ran, he couldn't. Some of his quickness seemed to have gone with the hood, and Crow had inherited it.

At last Crow called, "All right, you imp! Bargain. Make a flying spell for me, and I'll give you back your cap."

The elf stood still. "Sorceress! Cleery!" He looked around for her, and his face crinkled as if he were about to cry. "Make that silly rook understand, I don't know anything about magic weather. Elves don't make spells. Make him give back my hood!"

At that moment a small girl came running from the house. "Boy, what are you doing in my yard?" she called to Knobs. Then she saw Hodge. "Oh!" she shrieked. "What a cute little man!"

And before Cleery or Knobs could stop her, she scooped up Hodge and ran back to her house. They raced after her, but she slammed through the screen door, the elf kicking in her arms and trying to bite.

"Oh, for heaven's sake!" Cleery gasped.

"Now look!" Knobs exclaimed.

Crow, still invisible, came squawking along behind.

They'd have to rescue Hodge. But even in such trouble, Cleery gave a chuckle of pleasure. Now she could make good use of the invisibility cape. Gently she eased open the back door and stepped into the house. Down the hall she could hear the little girl's voice. "Stop that! Now be a nice brownie and play with me. Ouch!"

Cleery tiptoed down the hallway. Just then the housewife who'd been watching television came along it, and Cleery spread back against the wall, not to be touched. The woman glanced at the wall, as if she sensed the presence of something, and Cleery swallowed hard in order not to laugh. The woman went on into the kitchen, and Cleery went to the little girl's bedroom.

The child had stuffed the elf into a toy box and was holding open the lid just a crack to peek in at him. Hodge's power of unusual strength must have come from the hood, too, for he seemed unable to shove the lid up. Cleery could see his hands at the crack, pushing at the lid. Poor little elf! Cleery marched over to the box, not caring whether she made sounds, and pulled the lid from the child's grasp. Snatching Hodge up, she swept him under her cloak.

"Not for you," she said, and then, seeing the little girl's fright, she added more kindly, "Maybe you'll find your own magic someday."

She giggled, most unbecoming to an invisible fairy godmother. The thought made her laugh harder; Hodge joined in, and they chuckled their way out of the house.

Knobs was outside, the bird drooping on his shoulder, green hood in his hand.

Cleery touched Knobs and whispered, "Got him."

"Let's get out of here!" Knobs said.

They ran to the alley and headed for a thicket of trees and bushes farther along, where they'd be hidden. There Cleery took off the cloak. Crow sighed and looked the other way when the indignant elf came into view.

"Thank you," Hodge said hastily to Cleery and turned to the crow. "You!"

However, the bird was up on Knobs' shoulder, out of the elf's reach.

Crow hung his head. "Sorry."

Knobs still kept the little hood. "Now, let's get this straight," he said to Hodge. "You're a magic elf. Isn't there any way you can cure Crow's wings?"

Hodge shook his spiky head. "No," he said. "I just don't know how."

There was no teasing in the wrinkled face. Cleery and Knobs believed him. They both sighed heavily.

"All right. Here's your hood," Knobs said.

Hodge pulled it onto his head and grinned in relief. But he didn't disappear right away.

"Good luck," he told Crow unexpectedly. "Keep trying." He winked at Cleery. "It was fun. Now I think I'll find a place to rest. This cottage looks like a good possibility."

At the edge of the tangle of trees and bushes was a little house, set back by the alley. It was like a cottage tucked down in a forest.

Hodge winked again. "Good-bye." With a tug of the hood, he was gone.

"Crow."

Cleery took him onto her shoulder and looked at him. The inner lid of the bird's eyes filmed up and closed. Then the eye popped open, bright yellow again. Crow made a show of standing briskly on her shoulder.

"Wouldn't trust the magic of a tricky imp like that, anyway," he said.

"Huh!" Cleery said, smiling. She was so proud of him. She turned to Knobs. "Should we just go off and leave Hodge here?"

"Let's see what happens."

They pushed their way through the overgrown shrubbery and looked in a back window. Inside, they saw a cozy kitchen with a fireplace and a little white-haired woman sitting beside it, knitting. Despite the summer noontime, a small fire ticked away in the fireplace. On the hearth was the elf, lapping up milk from a bowl, while a cat stood by in a bristle of gray fur. Cleery remembered from tales that elves always looked upon a bowl of milk on the hearth as a sign of welcome. However, the cat thought otherwise. It spat at Hodge and leaped into the knitting on the old lady's lap.

"Here, here, what's this?" she said. She saw Hodge by the fire and nodded brightly. "Oh, company." She peered more sharply at him over her glasses. "Well, an elf. Well. Always hoped to see one. Hello there, sir."

Hodge nodded in turn. "Thanks for the milk."

A teakettle whistled from the stove. The old woman rose to hobble over to it, and it could be seen that she was quite crippled. Hodge motioned her back to her chair, saying he'd take care of everything. He scampered around the kitchen, brewing the tea, fixing a tray, and the grandmother exclaimed at how good he was. Hodge placed the tea tray on a stand by her chair, a nice little tray with two cups and a steaming pot on a doily. He laid a cushion on the hearth for the cat, brought a low footstool for the old lady's feet, and pulled up another stool for himself.

"One lump or two?" asked the grandmother.

"Never take sugar," said Hodge.

And then they had tea, while the cat and the little fire purred.

Cleery sighed, "Hmmm!" with satisfaction and smiled at Knobs.

He smiled back and nodded. "He'll be all right. Let's go."

On the way home, Cleery and Knobs decided to spend the rest of the day playing hide-and-seek with the invisibility cloak, not to waste its twenty-four hours of power. They could take turns, and it would be a challenge to catch an invisible person sneaking in free. But Cleery's thoughts turned back to Hodge.

"You know, Knobs," she said, "I'll never go into that alley again. Then there'll always be an elf in an alley of Cricklewood."

"Caw!" Crow exclaimed. "Deliver those poor people!"

Cleery only laughed. Not until the end of all the magic, she thought.

Witch
Magic

LITTLE BIRD-FOOTED MEN were dancing on Cleery's chest. Their feet tickled, and she laughed in her sleep, and that woke her up. She opened one eye and saw a beak in front of her nose. A yellow eye glared at her.

"Wake up!" Crow stood on her chest, righteously awake in the morning sunlight.

Cleery murmured, "Crow," her eye closing again. The morning was cool, and it felt good to drift back to sleep under the light summer blanket.

"Pay attention!" Crow tapped her nose with his beak, and Cleery's eyes flew open. "I don't think that mermaid knew what she was talking about. We've got to try something else."

"Mmm?"

But there was no point in trying to sleep with a crow pecking her and squirming his toes on her chest. Cleery shoved her pillow behind her and sat up in bed. Crow began to pace back and forth on the blanket.

"It's hit-or-miss, that's what. We've got to get organized." He thrust his beak forward to emphasize his point. "All this chasing around after some kind of silly weather! Tah. What I need is somebody with good, old-fashioned magic to fix me up. You hear?"

Cleery giggled. With his wings back, Crow looked like a little black man pacing with his hands clasped behind his back. Playfully she wiggled a toe under the blanket for Crow to pounce on as a kitten would. He gave the toe a nip that hurt right through the cover. Then he stamped to the foot of the bed and stood with his back to her.

"Nobody cares," he announced.

"Ah, Crow," Cleery said, laughing.

But she felt a twinge, because she didn't have any idea how to find the magic Crow needed. What if she never did?

"Look, Crow, it isn't so bad to be a magic crow," she coaxed. "Don't you enjoy it? I'll bet you're the only magic crow in the world."

The black bird stalked up the bed toward her. "How would you like to be a magic Cleery?" he demanded. "It's all very well to *use* magic and to see magic happening and to adventure off to magical places. Right?" He planted his feet on her leg and glared up at her. "But, you want to be you, Cleery, having the magical adventures. Right? So I want to be me, a regular flying crow!"

Cleery looked down at him. She remembered how she'd felt wearing the invisibility cloak. The cloak had been more than a gadget for being unseen, Cleery realized suddenly, and she ran her tongue over her lower lip thoughtfully. She'd felt transformed with lightness and gaiety, more like some hidden inside self. But for Crow the magic change hadn't been the same. In a way he was more of himself, yet in another way, less, crippled. She had never lost the ability to be all she was, but he had.

"I see," Cleery said.

Crow bobbed his head. "You bet your boots! I want to be what I'm supposed to be."

So, as soon as Cleery had washed the breakfast dishes, she put the magic box in her pocket, and she and Crow set off to get Knobs. They found him cleaning out the garage, whistling silently as he stacked some empty boxes.

"Knobs, you can't waste time doing this," Cleery said. "Come on. Crow's all upset."

Knobs shook his head. "Have to finish here first. My dad says this was the one job he wanted me to get done this summer and that I'd better hop to it."

Cleery helped Knobs so he'd be done sooner. While they were working, Crow practiced gliding. He had Cleery put him on a rafter, jumped off, and swooped down. "Look at me!" he would squawk. His spread wings helped him sail downward, but they wouldn't lift him when he flapped. Cleery had to stop often to put him back on the rafter.

At last the garage was swept and orderly. Knobs reported to his mother that the job was finished, filled a paper sack from her cookie jar, and they were ready for the alleys. At the corner, they considered which part of town to explore. The morning had grown warm and steamy, and Cleery and Knobs were perspiring from their work. It would be nice to find a shady alley. But Crow had other ideas. He complained again that the search for magic weather was a fool's chase. What he needed, he said, was a good old-fashioned magician. Knobs tried to remind the bird that the mermaid's prophecy was their only clue, but Crow was in no mood to listen to reason. He demanded to see the magic box.

Cleery eased it out of her pocket and held it up to him. Leaning forward on Cleery's shoulder, Crow passed his beak through the faint flicker of flame.

"Give me," he instructed fiercely, then stopped. The last bit was barely whispered, "Please, a magician."

Cleery looked at the old bird and smiled at him, her eyes soft. "I don't know about a magician," she said hesitantly, "but there's a part of town where some strange people live. You know, Knobs?"

He nodded, his face lighting up. "Billygoat Hill!

Let's go! Let's go!"

Billygoat Hill was across town, on the other side of a ravine. It was said that long ago a man had pastured his goats on the hill, but now houses straggled around it, following the rises and hollows, and only an occasional goat could be seen in a side yard. The houses were wooden cottages, some so old the foundations had settled, so that one part of a house sagged lower than the rest. Most of the people on Billygoat Hill were poor, but there was a wild tang to them that Cleery liked. Old Man Flinter lived over there, and he could actually draw with his toes. Cleery had seen him do it. A gypsy woman lived there, too. She didn't travel anymore. The younger men on Billygoat Hill worked now and then, but some people didn't seem to get up until afternoon. Once Cleery had seen a woman standing at her back door at noon, still wearing her bathrobe and yawning, as if she'd just waked up. Cleery and Knobs had explored Billygoat Hill before, because the alleys were fascinating. It seemed the poorer people were, the more interesting stuff they threw out behind their houses.

Cleery was hot from walking across town, so she led the way into a tree-shaded alley, even though she'd been in it before. The alleys weren't paved, nor were most of the streets. The dirt alley they had entered went crookedly up the hill, past backyard vegetable patches and tangles of junk. Cleery pointed to a framework of rusted bedsprings.

They'd been set on their ends to make a little three-sided house, with springs roofing across the top. Inside was a pedestal of sea shells cemented together. The open bedsprings didn't really provide shelter for the pedestal, and there was no reason to shelter it anyway, or even for the pedestal to be there, back by the alley. None of it made sense. That's what Cleery liked about it.

"It's still there," she said, pleased.

"Yes, and there's old Dobbin."

Knobs went over to a horse, behind the next house. The horse was gray with age and had a red bow tied to the end of its stringy tail. Maybe the better to switch flies with, Knobs had reasoned previously.

"Hi, Dobbin, want a cookie?" Knobs said. He touched a chocolate cookie to its lips, and the horse chewed it up, switching the red ribbon.

"Play, play, play, that's all they want to do!" Crow told the sky. "Never tend to business."

Cleery interrupted, whispering, "Look who's coming."

Up the alley trudged an old woman, pushing a baby buggy, which rattled and clattered, heaped with junk. The woman wore a man's hat stuffed down over a clump of gray hair, a ragged overcoat, despite the warmth of the day, and bedroom slippers flapping on her feet. One wheel of the buggy flapped, too, veering out with every turn, as if about to fall off.

"Baby Buggy Betty," Knobs breathed. He and Cleery retreated behind the horse, so the old woman could pass with the alleyway all to herself.

Baby Buggy Betty had lived in Cricklewood forever, so far as Cleery knew. She scrounged things in the town dump, behind houses and stores, wherever she could find things. She always pushed a baby buggy to carry the things she found, but no one could say what she did with the junk. Children told awful stories about her, what a mean temper she had and how scary she was. They'd shout at her, "Rubber baby buggy Betty," from the old tongue twister, calling it faster and faster, "Rubber-baby-buggy-Betty," and then "Rugger-bab-bubby-Betty," when their tongues stumbled. She'd shake her fist at them and yell back. Sometimes she'd yell terrible threats. One boy told Cleery, "She said she'd break off my arm and use it for a hammer and pound me three feet into the ground."

Cleery and Knobs never called names at her, though. Cleery rather liked her. Cleery's mother said Baby Buggy Betty was pathetic, and somebody ought to do something. But Cleery knew she wasn't pathetic. One time she'd come upon the old lady in the town dump, happily singing as loud as she could, "Glory, glory, hallelujah!" Cleery admired Baby Buggy Betty for the free way she lived, and she felt akin to her, hunting through the alleys for treasures.

As the woman came up the hilly way, she began

to sing, "Here comes old Sam Grinder—unh, get on, you buggy—with his old rusty gun—" She broke off when she saw Cleery and Knobs peering around the horse, and her wrinkled face creased into a grin. "That's right, hide, chickies. I might eat you!"

Cleery grinned back. She didn't think so. When the buggy clatter had gone over the rise, she said to Knobs, "Let's see where she goes."

They followed over the knob of the hill, at a safe distance, and hung back when they saw Baby Buggy Betty stop at a back door. "Here's that coffee pot you need, Freida," they heard her say to someone inside, as she rummaged a battered gray pot from the buggyful of junk. She paused again, to hand a peeling toy truck to a child, who was swinging in a rubber tire hung from a tree. Then she crossed a street and pushed her buggy into another alley that plunged down a hill. She stopped at the first house, whose back door was at the alley's edge. She called to someone through the screened door.

"How's your goat today, Jamie?"

In the yard beside the house, a despondent black goat stood with its head down, not eating.

"No better," a man's voice replied.

"I'll fix up a tonic for her, from my garden. Don't you worry, Jamie," the old woman said cheerily.

She went on, leaning back to hold the buggy from running away down the steep hill. Cleery and Knobs had loitered in the street while Betty had spoken to the goat's owner. Now they followed her into the alley. Suddenly the sky was dark with a purple cloud, a gust of wind brushed through the trees, and, curiously, sparks of lightning ran along a fence rail—curlicues, squiggles of lightning. Zinging, the lightning leaped from the fence to the old woman, just as thunder clapped. A flash. Cleery gasped. But Baby Buggy Betty still stood there, not struck dead.

Not dead. Changed. The overcoat billowed into a long black cape, and the woman seemed to hunch under it. Her old hat became white, the brim widened, the crown rose to a point. Baby Buggy Betty had turned into a witch.

Knobs was awestruck. "Changed, right before our eyes!"

"Knobs! I've never been in this alley!"

The witch-woman leaped onto the buggy atop the collection of junk. "Away!" she shrieked. The buggy rose a few feet off the ground and sailed down the hill, the witch clutching the handle with one hand and her white hat with the other, black cape blowing out behind. Cleery and Knobs watched the sight flying below the purple sky. They couldn't say a word.

"Ah now, a good, old-fashioned witch!" Crow said happily.

Knobs answered rapidly, "Well, a witch ought to be more help than Cleery'self." He was speaking so quickly, the last two words ran together. "Cleery's elf," he prounounced again.

Cleery looked at him. Slowly she said, "Elf. Self."
She and Knobs were silent.

"Hmmm," Knobs said. He looked at Cleery, and
for a moment she was aware of nothing but his
solemn eyes and her own staring back.

Then, "Come on, come on!" Crow squawked.
"What are we waiting for?"

As they ran down the hill, Crow flapping and
clinging to her shoulder, Cleery felt as if she were
looking into a glass pearled with mist, the mist
clearing away so that she could almost see. Knobs
had wanted to rescue a mysterious princess. Crow
wanted a magician, and here was the next thing to
it, a witch. When she'd used the cloak, she'd wanted
—Somehow the magic is tied up with us and how
we feel, she thought. And yet it's bigger, something
more than we can think up. She thought of the
heatless flame burning against her side in her
pocket and laid her hand on the box.

But now they had come to the witch's house. The
alley dead-ended in a hollow, at the bottom of the
hill. Trees stood thick in the hollow, and under
them was a wooden shack with a stovepipe jutting
out the back. Behind the shack was a clutter of junk,
but on the sunny side was a tangled garden. The
witch had wheeled the buggy into the shack and shut
the door after her. Cleery and Knobs picked their
way through the overgrown garden to a window on
the side of the house. Putting their noses to the

grimy glass, they peered through. Crow hopped in excitement, and his beak clacked on the glass as he looked in, too.

"Talk about junk!" Knobs whispered. "Baby Buggy Betty must have hoarded everything thrown away in Cricklewood for the last hundred years."

The interior of the shack fairly bristled with things. A heap of tools nested in an overstuffed armchair. A cot was littered with old hats and shoes. Stacks of magazines flowed out of every corner. Shelves lined a whole wall, every one laden with jars, cracked dishes, broken vases and figurines. At the back of the hut, stood a big, black iron cookstove covered with pots. Bending over one large enough and black enough to be a cauldron was the old woman. She muttered and waved her hands over the steam, shouted a word, pointed at the brew and looked into it.

"Pshaw!" she said, shaking her head.

She whisked some powder into the mixture from a shaker. Stirring up the brew, she chanted, pointed her finger, looked into the pot.

"Drat!"

"Maybe she can't make spells," Knobs said. "Maybe being a human, she isn't a full-fledged witch."

But Crow cried, "Try her. Try her!," so Knobs and Cleery went around to the door and knocked.

"Who's there?" said a gruff voice.

Feet stamped across the floor. The door opened, and Betty looked through the crack. Her nose seemed sharper, and her eyebrows were heavy as furry gray caterpillars.

"Don't need any children today." She started to shut the door.

Cleery stuck her foot into the crack and said, "Wait. Please, can you help us? My magic crow can't fly, and we need a spell to cure him."

"Spell? Hmph. To tell the truth, my spells aren't going too well today," said the old woman. "But come in, chickies." She pulled open the door.

Inside the hut, Crow got right to the point. "Are you a real witch?" he asked bluntly.

"White witch," she said, smacking the white hat down tighter on her gray curls. "I try to put things right for folks." She eyed the black bird with interest. "And you're a magic bird, eh, raven dearie?"

"I'm a crow, not a raven." Crow clucked worriedly to himself on Cleery's shoulder. "Rook, raven, they don't even know who I am."

Cleery stroked him. "I'm Cleery, and this is Knobs," she said.

"How-do." The witch-woman nodded. "I'm Witch Betty."

Even as a witch, old Betty didn't seem as scary as all the children said, only rather brusque. Knobs offered her the last cookie in the sack, and she ate it with gusto—"Chocolate icing, my favorite!"

Then they all went back to the stove to see about spells. Cleery was fascinated with the fine array of equipment that Witch Betty had. Lining shelves beside the stove were jars labeled: "Roast Bees," "Henbane," "Wolfsbane," "Powdered Toad," "Laurel Leaves," "Periwinkle," "Verbena," as well as many other herbs. It must have been the witch's herb garden they had seen at the side of the house. On the floor by the stove stood large china crocks, also labeled: "Bat's Blood," "Myrtle Branches," "Peewit's Blood," "Stag Beetles," "Bloodstones." A variety of birds' feathers stuck out of one jar, and Cleery hastily glanced away from an open crock labeled: "Wolf Eyes, Teeth, Feet."

"Let me just finish this brew," the witch said, flinging more powder into the black cauldron. "Then we'll see about the flying."

Someone had hexed Jamie's goat, she explained. Poor animal was bewitched and ailing. She was trying to make a potion that would break the wicked spell.

"But this brew won't jell," the witch complained. "Here, boy, hand me that mixing spoon."

Jell? Mix? *Oh,* Cleery thought. A smile tucked in at the corners of her mouth. It was amazing how things worked out.

Crow had thought of it, too, and he screeched, "Say witch, we've got just the thing. Here, Cleery, hand me that spoon."

So Cleery took the spoon from the box and gave it to Crow. Crow grasped the tiny silver spoon in his claw and showed the witch the tag that read, "Magic Mixing-Jelling Spoon."

"How about that for handy!" he said.

The woman took it doubtfully. "Pretty small for mixing."

However, when she put it into the brew, the trinket grew into a large spoon with a long handle, just right for stirring. Crow had Cleery perch him on a coffee pot next to the cauldron, to watch. Witch Betty stirred, and the mixture in the pot began to thicken at last. "Here we go," the old woman murmured. She nodded and grinned at Crow, as they bent companionably over the potful of magic.

Presently, though, Betty shook her head. "Still not right. It's supposed to turn into a clear liquid."

"Caw!" Crow cried impatiently. "Come on, brew, work!"

Immediately the brew bubbled and plopped, steam billowed, and the thick mixture shrank down to a shining liquid in the bottom of the pot.

"Raven, love, you did it!" The witch stroked the feathers of the black bird. "You're a regular witch's familiar, that's what you are. The cry of a magic bird, just the final touch my spells need."

Crow held his head proudly. "Good for a lot of things, you know."

The witch found a clean bottle, spooned the liquid into it, and stoppered the top. Then she begged Crow to help her with two more potions, before she made his flying magic. Her neighbors badly needed the cures, she wheedled. And she knew right where to find the flying recipe in her book.

"Flying recipe!" Crow blinked his yellow eyes and hopped from pot to pan.

"Righty!" she cocked her white hat back at a rakish angle, and went to work on another brew.

They all helped. Crow stood on the coffee pot, ready to caw at the right moment. Knobs fetched ingredients from the shelves and crocks, as the witch called them out, "Myrtle leaves—myrtle berries—henbane seed—stag-beetle oil—" Cleery stirred the mixture with the magic jelling spoon, and Witch Betty chanted strange words and waved her hands over the cauldron. This was to be an ointment to help Mrs. Tripp's chest complaint, the witch had said. Coughed something awful, her neighbor did. Right on schedule the brew thickened; Crow cawed, and the mess distilled into a green salve.

"Hurray!" Everyone laughed and congratulated each other.

The white witch bottled the salve, and they turned to the third concoction, a love potion for Cara. Cara was a sweet girl, who lived up the hill, the witch said, but Cara's boy friend had been ignoring her lately. The old woman consulted a thick book spread open on a table near the stove. The volume certainly looked old enough to be a recipe book of magic, its pages yellowed and stained. Betty flipped the pages.

"Love potion—love potion," she muttered. "This one? Let's see, 'Pigeon's liver, marrow of bones of wolf's left foot'? No. Ought to be herbs and flowers. Ah, here, 'Periwinkle, reduced to powder—' Yes, chickies, that ought to bring him around." She glanced at the children, eyes twinkling.

Cleery had shuddered at the part about wolf's marrow, and she was relieved that the ingredients weren't to be gruesome after all. Herbs and flowers sounded much more appropriate for a love potion.

Witch Betty sprinkled some dried blue peri- winkle flowers into the pot, ground them up and added a little powdered pearl. She let Cleery stir in the oil of roses, "For a delightful scent." She read from the recipe, then sent Knobs to the shelf for a jar of "All-Purpose Liquid Base." The mixture began to seethe and shimmer with color. Cleery mixed, the white witch chanted, Crow cawed, and a sweet odor came from the cauldron. In the bottom there appeared a pearly-blue powder. The witch scraped it up with the magic spoon and put it in a shaker-top jar.

"Now! Now!" cried Crow.

Witch Betty looked at him, hands on her hips, so that the black cape billowed out over her elbows. "We certainly work well together, raven dearie." She added rather reluctantly, "All right, now we'll make flying magic."

Again she consulted the recipe book. Not looking at Crow, she said, "Having had experience with

magic, I suppose you know flying takes a powerful magic, very hard to make."

There was something crafty in the witch's voice that made Cleery uneasy. The old woman began to call out the ingredients, "Wolfsbane, two blood-stones, powdered toad—"

As Knobs brought them to the stove, he whispered to Cleery, "Sounds more like black magic than white magic." She nodded, worried. But Crow hopped and flapped in a ferment of eagerness. He was about to fly!

Only he wasn't. The mixture jelled all right, and it turned to a black salve when Crow cawed happily. Witch Betty rubbed the ointment on his wings. Then when he sprang into the air from the stove, he thudded to the floor.

"My wings still won't lift!" he screamed.

He tried again and again, but he couldn't fly any more after the salve than he could before. The witch crouched down to the gasping bird.

"Now, dearie," she soothed, "we'll try again. The wolfsbane must have been too old. Herbs get that way. I'll just go out to the garden and gather some more."

While she was picking and preparing the herbs, Witch Betty asked, would Cleery and Knobs deliver the potions they'd already made. The cures were needed as soon as possible. She told them where the people lived, all of them within her block of alley, and gave instructions for the use of the charms.

Jamie was to rub some of the liquid behind his goat's ears, then bury the bottle where the goat liked best to graze. Cara was to sprinkle the powder on her beloved's food, and Mrs. Tripp should rub the green salve on her chest.

Cleery hesitated to leave Crow alone there. He looked so forlorn, clumped down on the floor. But Crow fluttered a wing at her.

"Go on," he said. "It'll work next time. Hurry back, so we can get on with it."

Cleery and Knobs took the jars and ran up the hilly alley. Over the hill hung the purple cloud, lightning flickering around its edges. Thunder muttered like the first threatening growls of an animal, and snatches of wind shook the trees, then left them motionless. Witch weather.

They found the girl and the ailing woman at their homes, and neither seemed surprised to receive Betty's tonics. Probably the old woman had made medicines from her herb garden, even before she turned into a witch, Knobs said. Cara did seem amused when she was told to sprinkle the powder on her boy friend's food. Her gloomy face turned to laughter and she promised to follow instructions, even though she said it sounded like witchcraft. Knobs and Cleery only smiled. At the goat's home, Cleery patted the miserable animal, while Knobs talked to its owner. The man had to be assured that the goat wasn't to drink the fluid, but he agreed to follow the instructions, too. Deliveries done, Cleery and Knobs raced down the hill.

Under the heavy sky, the air seemed closer. The gusty wind had stopped, and there was a breathless, waiting feeling to the air. Thunder rolled above, suddenly louder, and Cleery clutched Knobs' arm when the sound broke. Then as they neared the witch's house, they heard Crow cawing from within.

"Caw! Caw! Get me out of here!"

"Now what!" Knobs exclaimed.

The door to the shack was closed. It was locked. Knobs and Cheery knocked on it and rattled the handle.

The witch's voice called nervously, "Go away. No use. Some other time."

"It's Cleery and Knobs, your friends. Let us in."

There was no answer.

Cleery ran around to the window at the side. She could see Crow on the table by the stove. His feathers were ruffled with fury, but he seemed to be all right. The witch was bending over another steaming brew in the cauldron.

"Crow, what's wrong?" Cleery called.

The bird whirled toward the window. "She wants to keep me!" he shouted. "Forever. To make spells. And I think the flying magic failed because she doesn't want me to fly away." Crow's tongue showed in his beak, and his eyes glared.

The witch turned from the stove. "I couldn't help it," she said crossly. "Flying magic is too powerful for me to make. Now be a good bird and caw for this potion. Grampa Mitchell needs it."

"No!" Crow clacked his mouth shut and put his head under his wing.

Cleery pleaded with the old woman. "What's the matter with you? You're a white witch, a good witch. Why won't you help Crow?"

"Why are you keeping him a prisoner?" said Knobs, at the window, too.

Witch Betty stepped nearer to talk through the dirty window pane. Her wrinkled face was worried. "I told you why," she said. "I can't help the bird because I can't make the flying magic work." She coaxed, "Leave the magic raven here. I need him to make potions for the poor folk."

"No!" Cleery said. "You give me back my crow!"

"No!" The old witch's eyes shot a malignant look. "Go away, or I'll turn you into a toad."

Cleery drew back. She and Knobs hid behind a bush with reddish-black berries. All of the herb bushes were motionless in the tense air. Lightning glared, quickly followed by a burst of thunder.

"I don't think she can," Cleery whispered. "Let's break the window."

Knobs shook his head. The window was too small for either of them to get through, and it was the only one.

Things had taken a bad turn so abruptly that Cleery could hardly comprehend it all. They'd seemed so close to Crow's cure. And the witch had been so cheery, so helpful.

"What a shame!" she cried. "After all this, she can't make flying magic." She was close to despair. "Won't we ever find Crow's magic?"

Knobs' face was gloomy, too. However, he offered, "Well, an ointment isn't a weather of magic. Witch weather isn't crow weather. I guess we just won't find Crow's cure here."

"Then we've got to rescue him." Cleery sprang up and ran to the door. She pounded and kicked it. "Witch Betty, now you open this door!"

There was no response from within. Cleery continued to beat at the door. Knobs tapped her on the shoulder. He was grinning.

"Uh—Cleery, maybe if she weren't a witch anymore—?"

Cleery stared at him, then understood. She hesitated, looking at the locked door. Yet, if the witch couldn't make flying magic, there was no hope here. The alley went white with lightning, and thunder crashed, as she ran up the hill. Cleery stepped out of the alley. She entered it again. Suddenly the thunder and lightning were gone. The heavy clouds began to break up and wisp away, and the air felt lighter.

Down in the hollow, at the door once more, Cleery rapped gently. At once, feet stamped across the floor, the door opened, and Baby Buggy Betty looked out at Cleery and Knobs. Her white hat and black cape were gone. Cleery felt a pang of regret. And then—fright at the power she'd been given.

Behind Betty, Crow hopped down from the table and ran across the floor to the door.

The old woman smiled. "What's on your minds, chickies?"

"I—I just wanted my bird," Cleery said.

Crow scuttled past Betty, and Cleery caught him up.

"Well, forever more!" Betty exclaimed. "I was just wondering where that crow came from."

Cleery didn't explain. There was one thing more, though.

She said, "Miss Betty, when you were out finding things, I think you picked up my little silver spoon." It was a white lie. "I think that's it, on the stove."

The spoon lay on a pan beside the big black pot. The spoon was its dainty size again.

Baby Buggy Betty looked confused, then grinned. "Don't recall finding it, but I'm glad I did." She got the spoon and handed it to Cleery.

Then there was nothing more to do. Cleery looked at the old woman, a witch just a few minutes before. She said, "Well—thank you very much, Miss Betty. I—uh—really enjoyed it for awhile."

Betty gave her a puzzled look. "Sure enough, chickie. Come again."

Cleery looked back at the old woman for a long moment. "I will," she said.

Cleery and Knobs walked up the hill slowly. Crow had not said a word, but once they were out of hearing, he burst out in a fury.

"She deceived me! That was a pretty filthy way to act!"

Cleery tried to console him. "Don't give up hope. She was just being a witch, you know. I guess even a white witch can be—"

"Witchy," Knobs supplied.

Everyone was silent as they walked the rest of the way up the alley. Near the top they saw Jamie digging a hole in the ground, the bottle of clear liquid lying nearby. The black goat was eating grass and looked more perky already.

"I was wondering whether the potions would work, now that the alley isn't enchanted," Knobs whispered.

"Maybe we did a little bit of good," Cleery said, watching the goat start to frisk on the hillside.

Crow only said, "Huh!"

Kaleidscope Magic

MONDAY MORNING, Cleery's mother told her to come down to the store to get new school shoes. As Cleery walked along, a leaf fluttered down in the cool morning breeze. School shoes, falling leaves—time had come back into the timeless summer days. Summer was almost over. It ended next week, Tuesday morning, when school started.

And then the enchantments in the alleys would end.

Crow. Cleery had left him at home, and she thought of him glooming in her room. Even a witch had failed him. If the enchantments ended with the summer, according to her wish, then that meant no more chance for magic to set him flying. Her cocky bird would be weighted to the earth forever—

Of course, if he couldn't fly, she'd be sure to have him around always. Cleery put away the thought. She considered opening the pan of Last Magic. It was nearly the end now. Maybe the Last Magic would solve everything. But what if it didn't? Then she'd have nothing to help her in some last magical adventure in an alley. Only the rest of this week to free Crow!

At the store Cleery chose the first pair of shoes her father suggested, in a rush to get away. Then Mother said that after tomorrow she'd stay home to fit Cleery with school clothes she'd been sewing of an evening. She was surprised at Cleery's dismayed face. Fittings weren't that bad, Mother said, and Cleery tried to smile. Then she hurried away to find Knobs. Knobs' mother was helping the rush of time. She was making cookies in the shape of school bells.

Behind the house Cleery blurted out the urgency to Knobs. "—so we've got to find Crow's magic quick!" Knobs wasn't one to panic, but he agreed when Cleery said, "Let's hunt in every unexplored alley we can today."

At home, Cleery put only the round golden pan of Last Magic in a pocket of her jeans, and scooped up the bird.

"Come on. We're going to rampage all over this town today, until we find your cure!"

Crow perched on her shoulder obediently, but he stuck his head under a wing. "Won't do any good," he mumbled.

Cleery and Knobs went first to a new housing development on the edge of town. To their dismay, they discovered the area didn't even have alleys.

"Whoever heard of building a neighborhood with no alleys!" Cleery exclaimed.

Near the new houses, though, were some slightly older ones, and those did have an alley behind them. Cleery said she hadn't been there, so they entered the alley.

"I have," Knobs volunteered. "A mean kid lives in that house. And there he is."

Or was he? A fat boy ran into the alley yelling something, but his outline became smeary. He was shrinking, thickening, humping up, arms lengthening. His face stayed twisted in a scowl. His shout, "You can't go through my alley!" became, "Try to pass, and I'll eat you!" The thing's teeth were sharp and crooked. The boy had turned into a troll.

Cleery looked at the ugly creature in disgust. Crow looked once and put his head back under his wing. Cleery's eyes appealed to Knobs, so he took over.

"Troll, can you make flying magic for a bird who can't fly?"

The squatty thing growled. "I don't make magic. I eat!" It clashed its pointed teeth.

Cleery wasn't surprised. She hadn't expected such a hateful creature to be an agent for good. No point in wasting time there. She motioned to Knobs, and they went out of the alley the way they'd come. Stepping a foot back in, Cleery was glad to see the troll become only a fat boy again.

"Huh," Knobs said, smiling. "I ought to tell that kid what he'll turn into if he doesn't watch out!"

Then, as morning passed into afternoon, they hurried up and down the streets of Cricklewood, hunting alleys new to Cleery. In one, they saw something that in a way was even more grotesque than the troll. Four cats were crouched in an alley. As Cleery entered it, one gray tom rose on hind legs and began to direct the other cats. They opened their mouths and sang a caterwauling chorus. The tomcat and his choir looked rather funny, but Cleery shuddered. They were like a horrid cartoon of themselves. She backed out of the alley and put a foot in again to restore the cats to their natural selves. Crow was relieved. No cat would ever help a bird, he declared.

In other new alleys, Cleery did feel a certain charmed atmosphere, a weather of magic, and she thought of the mermaid's prophecy about Crow's weather. Strangely, the thought made her feel bleak —once Crow could fly, then—? She wanted him to fly. Of course! And yet—

At the bottom of a garden, enchantment touched a willow tree. The tree sang of lovely maidens and faraway places in a haunting sigh, and Cleery lingered to listen. There seemed to be no help for Crow there. In another alley, blowing leaves on the grass became a scurry of little pixie people. But the green pixies flew about playing pranks on each other and never would answer a word to Cleery.

As the three rushed through unexplored alley after unexplored alley, Cleery shook her head. So many enchantments in one day, like a kaleidoscope whirling before her eyes. Too much, too fast. She felt dizzy with magic. At last, she handed Crow to Knobs and drew apart from them, to drop down by a clump of daisies in the back of a yard. She had to be alone for a few minutes. Before, there'd been just one adventure in a day, with days in between to mull over the magic, time to experience finding something enchanted in an alley. Now there was no time to relish any of it.

Cleery looked around at the alley they were in, not sure whether she'd been there or not. It was like so many others, with their variety of trash piles and homey gardens. Next to a garage, across the way, was a heap of boards with some old bicycle parts thrown on top. Beyond, were rows of raspberry canes. Then in a tree she recognized a birdhouse, made like a castle with spires. She remembered seeing it once, in the spring, on an exploring jaunt, so that meant she wouldn't find an enchantment there. She felt relieved. She wouldn't have to face the possibility of some sudden adventure quite yet. It was hard to keep girded, ready to whirl into action to save Crow, alley after alley. She rested, idly pulling white petals off the daisies.

As she rested, she tried to sort things out. What were they looking for, anyway? She knew there was nothing physically wrong with Crow's wings, for she'd taken him to a veterinarian one day. So, what kind of power could help him? Crow's weather of magic, the mermaid had said. It sounded so vague. She didn't understand what that meant. At first, when she'd found the magical mermaid, she'd thought they'd have Crow flying in a minute. And when she'd seen the fantastic weather tower, she'd been sure. Ever since, they seemed to be getting further and further away from a solution. The ghost couldn't help Crow, the witch couldn't. What kind of enchanted creature could create a weather of magic? Where would a special weather of magic be?

Cleery pressed her fingers to her temples, for her head ached with strain; and as she moved, she saw Knobs squatting in the alley, drawing in the dirt with a twig. The black bird waited patiently beside him, beak drooping, eyes closed. Cleery took a deep breath and got up.

They rushed on, Cleery and Knobs and Crow. They didn't stop for lunch, and that made Cleery hungry and cross. The day had become dull and steamy, the sun breaking through the haze now and then to make the heat worse. Prickly weather. More alleys, more magic. From a garbage can, an ever-flowing cup, that poured out milk whenever it was tipped. From a rubbish pile, a hand mirror that reflected beautiful woodland scenery, but wouldn't show a flying spell for Crow. In the flames of an incinerator, a mocking imp who only repeated everything they tried to say to it. Cleery kept the cup and the mirror, for they might come in handy later, but she reentered the imp's alley to erase him from the flames. "Hateful little creature!"

As Cleery and Knobs went on, though, the cup and the mirror seemed to be infected with hatefulness, too. Knobs had to assume the chore of carrying the cup perfectly level, for it spilled milk down Cleery's legs when it was barely tilted. And the hand mirror began to show a succession of unknown children, all making faces at Cleery whenever she looked.

"What's wrong, Knobs?" she wailed. "It's as if the magic is trying to be just as mean as it can!"

Finally, from a trash heap in another alley, Cleery pulled out an old umbrella that lifted her from the ground in swoops. At that, Crow took his beak from under his wing, where he'd huddled most of the day.

"Even an umbrella can fly, but I can't," he mourned. Still, he sat on Knobs' shoulder and watched hopefully, as Cleery tried to control the wayward umbrella and perhaps learn some secret of flying from it.

Yet, the umbrella was the most mocking, hateful thing of the whole day. It seemed to lead a life of its own, not paying a bit of attention to what Cleery told it to do. As she clung to the handle, the umbrella jerked her up to a garage roof. Then it launched her toward a house chimney. She could hardly see, with the low afternoon sun glaring in her eyes, and she barely missed the chimney. "Stop! How can Crow fly?" she begged. The umbrella only jerked more viciously, lunged down, and crashed Cleery into a tree trunk. Then the umbrella folded itself neatly and lay on the grass, just as if it were harmless.

Cleery sprawled on the ground and rubbed a painful welt on her forehead. Frustrating! Everything in the day was frustrating and horrible. Cleery seized the umbrella.

"You mean hateful umbrella! I hate you!" She slammed the umbrella against the tree, jumped on it, smashed it to pieces. "Hate you!" She threw the pieces away.

"Now,—" Panting, she snatched up the mirror and grabbed the cup from Knobs' hand. The mirror showed her own face in a twisted caricature, and the cup spilled muddy water on her. It was like a nightmare. "Hateful! Everything hateful!" She threw the mirror and the cup to the ground, stamped on them, smashed them to bits.

Crow's beak hung open, and Knobs began, "Cleery, be sensible—"

But Cleery turned on him. At last, a human target for all of the day's frustration.

"Sensible!" she raged. "You're so sensible. All right, you take over! Here! I'm through!"

She thrust the gold box of Last Magic at him. Then she ran out of the alley, tears burning her hot face.

"Hateful!" she sobbed. "Everything!"

Including herself. Abruptly she dropped down on the curb across the street, covered her face with her hands and cried. Even when she had real magic, she couldn't handle it. She couldn't help Crow. She rocked on the curb, moaning, hiding her face in her hands.

"Don't cry." She felt the brush of a wing on her cheek. Small bird feet gripped her shoulder. "I'm getting used to not flying."

A hand touched her other shoulder, and Knobs eased down on the curb beside her. "Cleery," was all he said.

They sat on the curb in the late afternoon, nobody talking.

Cleery gave one last shuddering sob. The strain in her head faded, and quiet came over her. Knobs and Crow were with her. They wouldn't let her desert them.

Cleery lifted her face and swiped away the wetness with the heels of her hands.

"Well, there's still tomorrow," she said.

Last
Magic

DESPITE THE MISERY of the day before, when Cleery woke she had the feeling that something wonderful was going to happen. Yet it was mixed with the vague feeling of something strange, something almost frightening. Lying on her side, she opened her eyes and saw a pair of black legs striding past her nose. She watched, not letting on that she was awake. Crow jumped from the head of the bed to her dresser. He pecked among the things scattered on the top, then scratched at them with a foot. Cleery almost giggled. No wonder her dresser top was always a stirred-up mess. Crow found what he wanted, Cleery's green headband. He tugged it loose from the clutter, poised on the edge of the dresser with the ribbon in his beak, and launched out.

"Whoops!" he cawed, fluttering his wings to break the fall. He lost the headband when he cawed, but he pecked it up and strode off, with the green band bannering out from his beak. Into the closet he went and began twining the ribbon into his nest, on a side where the sticks were falling apart. "This is the way we *fix* our nest," he muttered, tucking away.

Such a dear, good Crow! Cleery smiled at him. She wished he could stay just as he was, her friend. Things were going to be different when he could fly. He would build a nest in a tree, not share her room anymore. And with that, in her first-awakeness, when truth shows up clearly, Cleery admitted the thing that had tormented her the day before: she didn't really want Crow to fly. Because then he might leave her.

Done with his nest, Crow stepped over to the chair by the window, hopped up, and onto the window-sill. He stood there, looking out at the morning. Bird song trilled in the freshness, and a robin flew past the window. Crow's beak opened, his wings lifted, then drooped, wing tips touching the window sill.

Poor Crow! She couldn't keep him captive. Cleery felt a pain in her chest, as if her heart really did hurt. She loved Crow. He had to fly. That's all there was to it.

Somewhere in Cricklewood there had to be one alley where an enchantment would appear to set

Crow free. But why hadn't they found the right magical creature? Or the right magical place? Their adventuring seemed so hit-or-miss. Or was it? Cleery remembered the hint she'd had when they'd seen the witch. Ever since the enchanted forest, each one of them seemed to find the kind of magic he really wanted. Cleery drowsed back toward sleep, while the idea swirled and expanded. Suddenly she sent a clear thought arrowing to the flame in her drawer: You know what kind of magic we need. Not what I choose—you make it.

Cleery was wide awake now. She turned onto her back, arms under her head, and began to think what kind of alley would be the very best. Then she sat up in bed. Instead of running out of summer, what if she'd already run out of unexplored alleys? Let's see, there was—no, she'd been there. Well, there was down by the box factory—no, she and Knobs had gone there in the spring, hunting through the industrial area for Reward signs and suspicious characters to report. Cleery wrinkled her nose, remembering the smell of rotten eggs behind the chicken hatchery. Oh, of course, there must be alleys left; she couldn't have walked in all of them. Cleery jumped out of bed, in a hurry to start looking for an unexplored alley. The something's-going to-happen feeling came back.

As Mother left the house, she told Cleery to clean up after Crow, she was tired of finding bird droppings all over the place. Cleery looked around indignantly, hoping Crow hadn't heard. It was such an *ordinary* thing to say, at the beginning of a magical day.

Knobs was waiting on his front steps, and he was glad to see Cleery happy again, eyes sparkling. Even Crow caught Cleery's hope. He rode her shoulder jauntily and snapped, "If you're going to skip, I'm going to be seasick," just like his old self.

As they walked along the familiar streets, Cleery took the gold pan from the box in her pocket. Such a light thing, fitting snugly in the palm of her hand. Once more she studied it, hoping for a clue as to the kind of alley she should seek. The jewels sparkled: "Last Magic." The last of the magic. Cleery held the warm gold against her cheek.

Knobs asked, "Is the flame still burning?"

Cleery looked in her pocket. Yes, there was the tongue of fire, even though she held the Last Magic, and all the rest of the magic things had been used. The flame—suddenly Cleery remembered something, the thing that had haunted her when she woke.

"I had a dream!" she exclaimed. "Just before I woke."

She told it. She'd seen the whole earth like a globe, with people standing all over it, shouting and singing. Above them, the sky flickered with golden tongues of fire, but she couldn't tell whether the flames were rising or descending.

Cleery's heart pounded with excitement, remembering. Then she realized that Knobs and Crow hadn't spoken.

At last Knobs said, "Cleery, I dreamed that, too."

"So did I." The crow's voice was low.

They all looked at each other.

The tension was too much for Cleery. She laughed. "I didn't know birds dreamed."

"Ha," said Crow. "Lot of things you don't know." But he brushed his beak through her hair.

They walked on. When it came to picking the right alley, Cleery found she'd been right. It was hard to find one she hadn't explored. They looked into the entrances of alleys, behind big, old homes, alleys behind expensive, new houses, alleys behind ordinary houses, until they found themselves on the edge of town, with the woods beyond. Just to make sure, Cleery turned down a short side street that dead-ended with the last house. And then there it was, another alley, an alley she hadn't known about.

It ran behind the last row of houses, and on one side were back yards and vegetable gardens, on the other side the woods. At one time, it might have been a road along the town limits, but now it was only an alleyway between the houses and the forest. Yet, the beauty of it! Cleery drew in her breath in delight. The lane was lined with trees on both sides, a woodland avenue, right at the edge of town. The first two trees, one in a back yard, the other in the woods, stood like gateposts at the entrance, and rows of trees stretched away, tall and old, trunks mossy green with age. Branches met over the alley, with shimmers of yellow in the green leaf canopy. On the dirt alley floor, fallen leaves spattered brightly. Cleery looked into the green tunnel and saw more, saw that this was the best alley of all. For the way rose up a gentle hill, and the rows of trees led to a patch of sky.

"You can't see the end of the alley," Cleery whispered. "Nothing blocks it off and makes an end to it."

Crow's voice was hushed, too. "I feel as though, if you'd fling me through there, I'd sail right on up into the sky."

Cleery turned to Knobs without speaking. He nodded gravely, and she entered the alley.

Beyond the trees, on the town side, everyday back yard life went on—a girl sunbathing, a child humming in a sandbox. Yet the alley seemed seldom used. Driveways from garages led out to the street in front. There weren't even any garbage cans along the way, so the garbage must be collected from the street.

Under the boughs, the lane was luminous with a green-gold light. Ferns feathered the ground around tree roots, and the fresh smell of greenery mingled with the cool dampness of old leaves going back to earth. There was a movement to the woods, a whirr of wings, the springing up of a branch, shaking its leaves, as a bird released it, the rush of a squirrel on a trunk. New-fallen leaves on the path were damask-smooth under Cleery's feet, the air warm where the sun filtered through.

Yet it was more than a beautiful, wooded alley. There was something else, a strangeness. As Cleery and Knobs walked, watching, the rustles in the woods became a pulsation, as if something vast were breathing through it all. The rhythm beat, built, clung to the edge of hearing, a climate of expectancy trembled in the alley.

Cleery looked through the trees to the back yards. Surely the people there felt it. But no one was in sight. She looked at Crow, at Knobs. Their eyes looked back, wondering.

They walked on, and then through the row of trees on the town side, they saw a figure. In a yard was a small corn patch, and among the stalks of corn, a scarecrow. The scarecrow was dressed in black: ragged black trousers, black coat, black hat, long-fingered black gloves. In the blackness, its face was a startling white, eyes and mouth painted on the white face. The scarecrow stirred, the glove fingers writhed like black worms, the coat flapped in the breeze.

But there was no breeze.

The black trouser legs moved—the scarecrow-man began walking.

"Horrible," Crow whispered. He crouched on Cleery's shoulder.

This is the enchantment, Cleery told herself. It couldn't be! It was evil. It was the worst kind of creature, made to threaten, to harm Crow, not help.

She stood, one hand flung up to the bird, the other clenching the gold pan. And then she recognized the scene. She'd dreamed it, too, a dream deeper in the night. There had been a black scarecrow walking, walking, looming close to her, painted mouth stretching wide, worm-fingers reaching for her—and Crow flying to attack. *Crow flying!*

Cleery pried open the lid of the gold pan. Inside, a white powder. And letters engraved on the underside of the lid, words that read: "To make a dream come true."

The figure rustled as it walked, tramped slowly to the edge of the trees. There it stopped, stood swaying, terrible blank eyes fixed on Cleery.

She whimpered.

"I'm just a girl. I can't—"

"To make a dream come true." A nightmare. What did the Thing do to her?

And yet—Crow flying!

"All right!" Cleery cried. She pinched up the powder and threw it in the air, shook the boxful of powder into the green-gold light. "Come on!" she shouted.

The eyes stared, the scarecrow-thing began its slow walk, walking out into the alley toward Cleery. Knobs clasped her hand, "What—"

"Cleery-girl," Crow's voice rasped. Shuffling, rustling, the creature drew near. A hissing came from the painted mouth, as the arms lifted and the glove fingers reached.

There was a stir in the trees, and a sigh of air lifted the leaves. A wind was coming, a sudden gust of wind sweeping through the woods. Crow stood taller on Cleery's shoulder, "Hello?" The wind swirled through the trees, bending them, shaking them, blowing Crow's feathers wrong side out. "Yes!" he cawed. "Yes!" It was a crow's wind, pitch-falling wind, high-soaring, March-sky-scouring wind. It was a mighty wind rushing.

The white face loomed, black fingers seized Cleery's throat. She screamed. And Crow sprang away from her shoulder.

He sprang into the wind, cawing, clawing at the scarecrow, flapping to dig at the eyes, bite at the fingers. One black hand groped for the crow.

"Run!" he cawed. "Run out of the alley!"

Cleery obeyed. Her feet digging in the dirt, she ran on through the alley, and the wind blew with her, skimmed her along, sang in her ears. She looked back. The scarecrow was running after her, mouth hissing. Knobs tried to grapple with it. Crow flew around the creature, flapping, pecking, cawing. Cleery ran. And, at last, another side street ended at the wooded lane. It was the end of one block of alley. She sped into the street, whirled, darted back toward the scarecrow.

It collapsed. The evil thing was nothing but a

heap of old clothes and straw on the alley. Knobs panted, looking down at the heap. Crow wheeled and cawed above it.

"Crow!" Cleery called up to him, heaving for breath. "You can fly!" She wanted to hug him and sob with happiness.

Still the wind rushed through the woods, every tree and fern moving, rustling with its power. Crow swooped and rose on the wind. "Caw!" he cried.

"Crow, come here."

He flew over her head, circled, looked down at her. The yellow eye, glancing, was not the eye of a friend. It was instead the eye of a bird.

Cleery reached. "Crow!"

The bird fluttered up. Yet it circled once more, and a black feather fell down on the wind, whisking, dropping at Cleery's feet. Then the crow winged straight along the avenue of trees and called a triumphant "Caw!" Between the trees the bird swept on the wind up into the blue at the top of the lane, a black speck sailing high against the sky.

"Crow?"

An ache came into her throat. Yet she stood gladly in the wind, for it was Crow's weather of magic. It was a mighty wind rushing, the very breath of Magic, that could enter into anything and make it what it was meant to be. To see this mystery happen—Cleery trembled with the joy of it.

The joy, so poignant, changed to a remembered feeling. Cleery stooped and picked up the black

feather, smoothed its crispness.

Knobs stepped near and touched her shoulder. "Cleery?" His face was white, and his eyes blinked as if a sudden brilliance had passed in front of them.

Cleery's eyes shone with tears. "The wonder— Crow—"

As they stood in the alley, the wind passed away through the lane of trees, into the sky beyond. The leaves stilled on the trees. The window of sky belonged to Crow. They turned and walked back the way they'd come.

Knobs said, "Cleery, there are still good alleys to explore. Even though summer is done, there are still Saturdays and alleys."

She smiled at him. "I know." There were still alleys, still Knobs, she still liked being Cleery.

Something pressed her palm, something besides the feather. She saw she was clutching the gold pan, and she looked at it once more. Yes, the powder was all gone. But there, pasted on the bottom, hidden before by the powder, was a faded scrap of paper. Instructions were printed in an ancient script: "Deliver all to a shop in the next town west."

Cleery looked at the words for a long time; Knobs, too. How long, how many times had the box and its flame been passed on, westward? How many times had the magic renewed itself for each finder? So many people using the magic—Who?

A child, a knight, perhaps a lonely old lady, finding adventures by the way they used the contents of the box. All the magic that had happened, all the people who had walked in a weather of magic.

Cleery said, "We'll pass it on, Knobs. There'll still be magic in the world."